P9-DZN-287

Gates of Eden

Gates of Eden

stories

ETHAN COEN

ROB WEISBACH BOOKS
WILLIAM MORROW AND COMPANY, INC., NEW YORK

Published by Rob Weisbach Books
An Imprint of William Morrow and Company, Inc.
1350 Avenue of the Americas, New York, N.Y. 10019

Three stories first appeared, in slightly different forms, in the following publications:

"The Boys" in *The New Yorker*
"Gates of Eden" in *Playboy*
"A Fever in the Blood" in *Vanity Fair*

It is the policy of William Morrow and Company, Inc., and its imprints and affiliates, recognizing the importance of preserving what has been written, to print the books we publish on acid-free paper, and we exert our best efforts to that end.

Library of Congress Cataloging-in-Publication Data
Coen, Ethan.
Gates of Eden : stories / Ethan Coen. — 1st ed.
p. cm.
ISBN 0-688-15914-1 (alk. paper)
I. Title.
PS3553.0348G38 1998
813'.54—dc21 98-20853
CIP

Printed in the United States of America

First Edition

1 2 3 4 5 6 7 8 9 10

BOOK DESIGN BY RENATO STANISIC

www.robweisbachbooks.com

CONTENTS

Gates of Eden

DESTINY

Irv Chartaris clapped me on the shoulder as the bell sounded and I skipped out toward the center of the ring. Balboni was walking in, keeping his head low and bobbing even when he was well back out of reach, like all lousy fighters do to show that they know the moves. When I got to him his right fist appeared. I guess it hit me; it was very sudden. Then immediately his left fist swung up but that one I saw. It hit me—I was so surprised by the right that I couldn't quite duck the left—but at least I'd seen it coming, so I felt good. Then I think he hit me with the right again, a couple of times, a thip-thip rhythm. None of this hurt really because it was happening so fast, but I thought, Jesus, he's getting me in a hole . . . I gotta—we've gotta get this fight started, but while I was thinking this he was hitting me. I'm not sure what came after the two jabs: more hits—lefts, rights, that was pretty much his repertoire. I started to say "Wait a minute!" because it didn't seem fair, all the hitting when I wasn't set, but I don't know if I got the words out. I heard Chartaris's voice—"Hands up,

Joey!"—and I did try to raise them, but then I had to throw them back for balance because the ring was tipping away. The one solid hit I remember taking was just then, when my hands were flung back and my hips were thrust out for balance because the damn canvas was about to swerve out from under me, and the son of a bitch Balboni picked that one vulnerable moment—WHOMP—to land a hard one in my gut. I couldn't breathe after that, which threw my whole fight plan into a cocked hat, relying as it did on breathing. So things started to go downhill.

"One bad fight, kid. You'll bounce back. You're young! You're a baby! Remember, kid, it's just one in the loss column. Just one fight."

"I'm not sure, Irv. 'Fight' implies an *exchange* of blows."

"That's good, kid. You got a sense a humor; that'll see you through the low points. And you're educated; just listen to ya talk, just listen to ya, will ya? What did I tell ya, kid? Did I tell ya fighting is a mental game? Being mentally on the ball—you got that. You got a leg up there on these other bums. A good leg up. Now this fight—"

"This beating."

"Heh-heh. This fight—"

"No no, really. It was a beating."

"Heh-heh. Okay, this beaten, kid. You know what the problem was?"

"Tell me."

"You were thinkin' too much. I mean, he's there, he's hittin' ya, ya can't *think* about this, Joey, it takes too long."

"I thought you said it was a mental game."

"In a sense, yes. But primarily, no. Primarily, you gotta hit the guy."

"Uh-huh."

"And that's where he beat ya, Joey."

"Uh-huh."

"With the hitting."

"Right."

"But this—I reiterate this, kid—not to feel bad. It's just one fight."

"Beating."

"Beaten. 'Cause I don't care who—Joe Louis, Joe Louis had the occasional bad fff—beaten. Joe Louis had the occasional loss, kid."

"Irv, I'm no historian of boxing, but I believe even in the course of losing a fight, Joe Louis would sometimes hit the other guy."

"May be, kid. I too am not a historian. But they still went down as losses, didn't they, kiddo? One in the loss column—just like yours. Huh, kiddooski? Joe Friggin Louis. JFL."

Irv had left and I was buttoning my shirt when the stocky man came in.

"Ah, look, it's Bagadonuts. Look at ya, ya fuckin' Bagadonuts, you're a fuckin' Bagadonuts, fuckin' look at ya." He shook his head. "Sheesh."

"Have we met?"

"Have we met. Have we met. Ya fuck ya, *no* we ain't met

ya fuckin' Bagadonuts. Benny. I'm a friend of Marty Stricklan's. I says to—"

"How *is* Marty?"

"Shut the fuck up. I says to Marty, look I need someone for a job, someone with a touch, you know, nice, not a fuckin' jerk, don't need no skills but not a jerk. And definitely—not a jerk. So he tells me he's got a nephew Joey who's 'lookin' for himself.' " The stocky man's head started shaking, and then his body as well. It looked like a stroke. His mouth fell open and the sound—larrlarrlarr—of a garbage disposal gurgled out. I realized it was laughter when his jaw slapped shut and he continued: " 'Lookin' for himself.' Course, he didn't tell me the reason you was lookin' for yaself was cuz yas a fuckin' Bagadonuts. Larrlarrlarr. Well, who gives a flying shit. I don't need no one beaten up."

"Uh-huh. Well, what *do* you—"

"Shut the fuck up. I got a personal situation. I got a wife here fuckin' someone else. His dick. Her pussy. Woom-pah woom-pah woom-pah. Do I gotta draw yas an illustration?"

"No."

"No. Course not. We're adults. My wife. For richer, for poorer, for sickness, for health, forsakin' all others, but not for fuckin' some lowlife fuckin' son of a fuckin' bitch. Huh?"

"Uh-huh."

"*Huh?*"

"No."

"*Fuck* no. Not in *my* fuckin' book. So ya see it's delicate. My wife gettin' bangarinoed by a business associate. Woom-pah woom-pah woom-pah. And I bet she screams when he gives it to her. Like a fuckin' Chinaman at the track." Here, with a haunted stare, he lapsed into silence.

Then he shrugged. "Well, what's the diff. So I got a divorce action. Which my position would be helped innumerably if I had proofadis. And this is where I talk to Marty. Seekin' *his* counsel. Seekin' *his* suggestion. Seekin' someone, an individual, a person not a jerk. Huh?"

"Uh-huh."

"*Huh?*"

Stumped, I said nothing.

The man Benny glared at me. Then he belched. Then he frowned, his gaze drifting away, as if wondering who had belched. Then he looked back at me and his eyes crinkled and his jaw dropped open. "Larrlarrlarr. Yarl right, kid. Fuckin' Bagadonuts."

Pictures. Benny Benedeck wanted pictures of his wife in the act with his "business associate" Lou Argo. He himself adopted the grotesque straining facial expressions he imagined they displayed during the act of sex, and told me to be sure to photograph their faces. Then he burst out laughing. He told me he would pay me two hundred dollars. Then he wept.

It wasn't a very attractive proposition and I asked for a day to think about it. But when I weighed my future, I had very little to throw onto the boxing side of the scales: I could promote myself as The Human Speedbag. I could print up business cards:

"JOSEPH CARMODY—BLOWS ABSORBED." I could adopt the professional name Harold "Happy" Landings and rent out advertising space on the soles of my shoes.

I called Benny and told him I was in.

He loaned me a Nikon camera and gave me a hundred-dollar advance. "They go to the Valley View Motel."

"You already know where they go?"

"Yeah, I had a private investigator follow her and establish the whatnot."

"Well—why didn't he take the pictures?"

"Money, kid. What's widdese questions? He's expensive. I figure once he gets things figured out, any schmuck can take the pictures. Widall due respect."

"Uh-huh. Yeah. It should be easy enough to get pictures of 'em going into the room. The motel room, there."

"Yuh-huh."

"Wouldn't that be enough to prove that they're, uh . . ."

"Wuddya sayin'?"

"Well, how'm I supposed to get pictures of them actually—"

"You gotta get 'em doin' it."

"But I'm not sure I—"

"THIS AIN'T A FUCKIN' NEGOTIATION! I WANT PICTURES OF 'EM DOIN' IT! I WANNA RUB LOU ARGO'S FACE IN HIS OWN SMELLY SHIT!"

"Okay, Mr. Benedeck."

"YOU HEAR ME?!"

"Yes, Mr. Benedeck."

"HIS OWN SMELLY SHIT!"

"I hear you, Mr. Benedeck."

He stood there panting. Suddenly his jowls quivered, his eyes rolled back in his head, and he clenched his fists. "YAGGGHH! THAT FUCKIN' FUCKIN' FUCK LOU ARGO! NNRRNPHH!"

It was hot in my parked Volkswagen. The car door burned when I tried to rest my elbow in the open window, so I sat with my hands moldering in my lap and felt my armpits turning slick.

I was parked on the street behind the Valley View, which was in fact in the Valley, not above it, and therefore had no view. My street was perpendicular to the motel's arcade of rooms. I could see the lot and anyone approaching any room. At midday the lot was empty.

The first car to pull in was a late-model Cadillac Sedan De Ville. Its air conditioner, I deduced, was going full bore, for the woman who stepped out was wearing a knee-length fur. She was tall—taller than Benny—and in her mid-forties, with dark glasses, rouged cheekbones, and a pruny mouth. She wore heels and tight pants that made her wriggle down the walkway like a small hoofed animal trying to shake a bur off its hindquarters. She held a key with a big plastic tag up by one ear and a purse in her other hand, and gave them both short, vicious wags for balance as she hastened toward a room, sneering at nothing in particular. She didn't look back at the Caddy's driver, who followed.

Lou Argo was fiftyish. Even from a distance I could tell that he'd had virulent acne as an adolescent, or else smallpox, or came from a neighborhood where the toughs fought with knitting needles. I eased the focus ring on the Nikon to where things swam to crisp and started snapping. I got Mrs. Benedeck walking, I framed over and got her walking with Lou Argo walking behind, I got her hunched with her key at a door midway down, I got her entering, I got him entering.

I got out of my car. It was good so far, but now came the tough part. I would give them a few minutes to get started and then give the knob a try. If it turned I would lunge in, take a few pictures, and sprint. I counted on Lou Argo not to pursue barefoot and naked; if he stopped to put on shoes, let alone clothes, I would be long gone. If the knob did not turn I would give the door the shoulder. If that didn't work, and I assumed it wouldn't, I'd have shot my wad and would just have to present Benny Benedeck with what pictures I had. They weren't bad, after all, and perhaps I would catch him in a good mood, though that of course was a roll of the dice.

But when I drew near the room I saw that I was in luck. Its front window had a vinyl-backed curtain which, though closed, hung away on one side—enough, as I saw when I stooped to peer in, to give me a view inside. Lou Argo was sitting on the bed with his back to me, hands up at his throat, either calmly strangling himself or else taking off his tie. Mrs. Benedeck was not in sight. I heard water running. From the layout, clearly, the bathroom was at the deep end of the room, adjacent to a vanity table and sink.

Well, this was good. I would get a moving blanket from the trunk of my car, tent myself off to keep my side of the window dark, and—

"What you doin'?"

A maid had backed her cart out of a room two doors down. She was a black woman in a tubular white uniform ensheathing rolls of fat. "That's a private motel room. What you doin'?"

I held up a quieting hand and trotted over to her. "It's okay." I thought about money. My wallet held the two fifties Benny had given me and a twenty of my own. "It's okay, I—I do this professionally."

"Do what now? That's a private motel room."

"It's okay." I took out my wallet. I tilted it away from her as I fished out the twenty so that the fifties wouldn't give her ideas. "It's okay, I'm not disturbing anyone. No one's going to know."

"Well," she quickly took the bill but frowned at me, "check with Mr. Curtis."

"Who's Mr. Curtis?"

"In the office."

"But—what if Mr. Curtis says no dice?"

"I can't help that!"

"Then what about the twenty?"

"I can't help that!"

"But why does Mr. Curtis need to know?"

"He's the manager!"

"But—if he's the one who decides, how come you get a twenty?"

"That's a private motel room!"

"I know, but—"

"Are you givin' me the sass?"

"No, not at all, I just—"

"Go check with Mr. Curtis!"

"I know. I will. I just—if he says no dice—"

"I can't help that! Are you givin' me the sass?"

"No, ma'am, I—"

"Go check with Mr. Curtis!"

She watched as cursing quietly, I crossed the lot to the office. Inside a man sat behind a counter watching a baseball game on a small black-and-white TV. He wore glasses with thumb-thick lenses and heavy black frames. The frame arms tension-gripped either side of his head and pulsed at his temples. He had a white crew cut and his ears too sprouted white hair. A clear plastic tube, taped to his upper lip with a butterfly bandage, snaked into one nostril. Its other end trailed down out of sight below the counter.

"Mr. Curtis?"

He looked up, nose tube swaying.

"I, uh, I've been hired to gather evidence, uh, in a certain official court case, involving a certain party who's rented one of your rooms here?"

He stared at me.

"So, I've got to just take a few pictures, which is perfectly legal of course, but the maid there suggested I get your okay. Of course, uh, I don't mean to put you out; if twenty dollars would make it all right, then I could certainly provide that for you."

He stared at me. Then he raised something that looked like a small hand blender to his throat. It went on with a click, and his speech came out with an electronic buzz: "GOKAY."

I took out my wallet. "Um"—I put one of the fifties on the countertop—"do you have change of a fifty?"

He took the bill, stuck it in his pocket, and went back to watching the ball game.

I watched him for a moment. "That was a fifty, sir—um . . ."

He made no sign of having heard.

"Sir, could I get thirty dollars back?"

With his eyes on the television he brought the hand blender back to his throat: "GUCK YOU."

"But—that was a fifty, sir."

"GUCK OFF, GYOU GLITTLE GASSHOLE."

My mood, so bright after taking those first pictures, had turned sour. Yes, perhaps the pictures of his wife engaged in the act would please Benny sufficiently not to demur at the extra seventy in expenses. But the man was so damned unpredictable, and I didn't want to be doing this job for $130. I was still cursing, and sweating heavily, when I returned to the motel-room window draped in a blanket from my car.

I heard noise from inside. They were at it; it looked like I was in gravy.

"AAAH! AAAH! LOU!"

It was missionary position—classic stuff.

"OH YEAH!"

"AAAH! LOU! SWEET BABY LOU!"

"AAAH!"

Mrs. Benedeck was flouncing up and down on the bed as if high voltage were coursing through the springs.

"SWEET BABY LOU! AAHHH!"

"AAAHH! BENNY BENEDECK!"

"AHHH! AHHH! LOU!"

"I'M DOIN' THIS TO *YOU*, BENNY!"

"LOU!"

"I'M FUCKIN' *YOU*, BENNY BENEDECK! AAHHH!"

"AHHH!"

Lou Argo waved a fist in the air: "I'M FUCKIN' *YOU*, BENNY! AHHH! AHHH! AHHH!"

"AAAHH! LOU! THE WINDOW!"

"THIS IS FOR *YOU*, BENNY! AAAAAHH! FEEL THIS, YOU PRICK! OOOHH! JESUS! JESUS!"

"NO! LOU!"

"AAHH! YES!"

"LOU! NO! THERE'S SOMEONE AT THE WINDOW! AAHH!"

I'd gotten plenty, and anyway, it was unbearably stuffy under the blanket. I flipped the camera strap onto my neck and was getting to my feet and starting to undrape myself when a sharp downward blow smashed my fingers through the blanket.

My arms dropped. A second blow hit my head. It had the sweet resonant sound of metal, dulled by the blanket. I stepped, stumbled, my feet tangling the blanket. I was falling.

I banged awkwardly onto the cement walkway. Blows continued to fall. I rolled onto my back and raised my forearms under the blanket. Blows crunched against them. I heard a door opening.

The blanket was yanked away. Stale air grew fresh. I was looking up at the fat maid swinging a vacuum cleaner pipe down at me. It cracked my upraised arm, no longer cushioned by the blanket. Next to the maid stood Lou Argo, dropping the blanket, his pocked face beet red, his erection rapidly waning.

The maid's white cap was askew and her tongue stuck out as she two-handedly raised the pipe, as if to split rail. The pipe's hose waggled behind. I rolled onto my hands and knees and tried to crawl away as the pipe whooshed down and cracked my spine, and Lou Argo kicked upward into my ribs.

"YOU . . . FUCKIN' . . . PUNK!"

"I CAME SOON AS I HEARD YOU BEIN' DISTURBED, MISTUH ARGO!"

"UNGH! FUCKIN' PUNK—UNGH!"

The kicks stopped and I felt fingers close over the camera strap at the back of my neck. The strap was yanked, and the camera slammed into my face.

The pipe hit my back again.

"HE'S A RASCAL! HE'S A LITTLE PEEPIN' TOM, HE IS!"

I kept crawling and the pipe slammed into my ass. The camera was yanked into my face again. The pipe hit my ass again. The pipe gave a tonal whoosh each time it was swept against my ass.

"HE'S A RASCAL! UNGH! HE'S A—UNGH!—HE'S A TRICKY ONE, MISTUH ARGO!"

Fingers from behind dug into my scalp and yanked my hair. My neck stretched back. I gurgled. I felt a bare foot plant on my back for leverage, and the camera strap was yanked like a lawn mower cord, smashing the camera back into my face. But now one strap clip broke and tinkled to the pavement as the camera swung away free. The fingers let go my hair.

The humming pipe warned me to clench my ass each

time it was about to hit, but a heavy blow to the back of my head came from nowhere. Lou Argo was whipping me with the camera.

He yelled, "FUCK YOU, MURIEL! FUCK YOU!"

The maid yelled, "MY NAME AIN'T MURIEL, MISTUH ARGO!"

Lou Argo yelled, "I KNOW THAT! UNGH! TELL MURIEL TO GO TO HELL!"

"UNGH! I DON'T KNOW NO MURIEL, MISTUH ARGO!"

"I KNOW THAT! UNGH! I'M TALKIN' TO THE PUNK!"

I stopped trying to crawl away and curled up as they kicked, swung, and hit. The last thing I saw, as I tucked my head into my arms and wondered who Muriel was, was Mr. Curtis, the manager, watching from across the lot, arms folded, leaning against the jamb of his open door, his tube glinting in the sunlight as it swayed between his nose and the dark of the office interior.

"Muriel is Lou's wife," Benny Benedeck explained over lunch. "I guess he thought Muriel sent you—heh-heh-heh. Boy, he beat you up pretty good!"

I didn't think my stock would rise if I told him that the maid had helped. I was relieved, though; Benny was taking it much better than he might have. He didn't seem at all disconcerted that I had no pictures to offer. Perhaps it was my battered face, which greatly amused him; at any rate he ostentatiously told me to order anything at all from the menu. It was a nice Italian place where everyone seemed to know him. I suspected that in spite of his name, Benny himself was Italian. He was in a good mood; I dared to ask.

"Oh sure, kid. Alfonse Beneditto, that's my real name."

"Alfonse—like Capone?"

"Gyagyagyagyagya!" Benny trembled with laughter. "Gyagya keesh! I love this kid. I love this fuckin' kid. That's right, kid, like Al Capone."

"And Mr. Argo is a—he's a Mafia figure, isn't he?"

"Gyagyagya. 'A Mafia figure.' I love this kid. 'A Mafia figure.' What's a friggin' Mafia figure?"

"Well, you know—"

"If a guy knows some guys, is at make him a Mafia figure?"

"So . . . Mr. Argo knows some guys?"

"Sure he knows some guys. *I* know some guys."

"But I, for instance, don't know some guys."

"No, kid. You don't know some guys."

"Uh-huh. And that's why the private investigator didn't care to take the pictures, once he determined whom your wife was . . . dating. Not wanting to incur Lou Argo's wrath."

"Yeah, right, he didn't wanna incur any wrath. He was no dumbbell."

"Unlike me."

"Gyagyagyagya. Speakin' a which, kid, in all seriousness, I still need those pictures, so when was yas contemplatin' climbin' back on that horse?"

I stared at Benny. He returned an attentive smile.

I told him it was impossible. I described the flukelike circumstances that had given me my opportunity, so unlikely to recur, and even less likely now that Lou Argo would be on his guard, and, worse still, on his guard against *me*. I told him that I thought another attempt on my part to photograph Lou Argo having relations would lead only to another beating, or worse. I told him—but Benny's look was growing sour, and he waved a dismissive hand:

"Aaahhh. So you're tellin' me I can't count on you for this then?"

"I'm sorry, Mr. Benedeck. I just don't think it's safe for me now, and besides, maybe the case needs some fresh blood—a new approach—"

"Ah f'Chrissakes. F'Jesus fuckin' Jesus—ah, ya dumb fuckin' Bagadonuts." This epithet no longer held its gently ribbing tone. Benny darkly murmured, "Ahright, forget it. Fuck it. Forget it. Gimme back the hundred bucks I advanced ya, and the camera."

"But—Mr. Benedeck! I had to give away seventy bucks, like I told you, and the camera—"

"I DON'T GIVE A SHIT! I WASN'T PAYIN' YA TO GET BEAT UP!"

"But—Mr. Benedeck!"

"THAT'S ALL YA FUCKIN' DID!"

"But—Mr. Benedeck!"

"ARE YOU SAYIN' I GIVE YOU A HUNDRED BUCKS AND A THREE-HUNDRED-DOLLAR CAMERA AND ALL YOU WANNA GIMME BACK IS THIRTY FUCKIN' BUCKS?!"

"No, of course not—"

"ARE YOU JERKIN' ME OFF?!"

"No, of course not—"

"HUH?"

"No no, Mr. Benedeck, I assure you. It's just that I don't

have the, uh, the, uh—that would be four hundred dollars then?"

Benny stared at me, sucking breath in and out through his open mouth.

"It's just that I don't have the four hundred bucks on me. At the moment."

Benny stared.

"Of course I recognize that I owe it to you. That's a given. I just don't happen to have it. On me."

Benny stared. His breathing grew more regular. At length he said: "I didn't mean right this minute. Ya fuckin' screwball." He looked down at his plate of pasta fagioli as if noticing it for the first time. He frowned. He looked about the table, found a spoon, and started eating. He said through a mouthful of food and without looking up, "Just get it to me inna week."

"Okay. No problem." I got up, hesitated. "Actually—I don't have quite that amount—I can get it, I know right where I can get it—but . . . what happens if it takes a little more than a week?"

Benny was shoveling in spoonfuls of pasta fagioli. "Then I have someone beat the livin' fuckin' shit outa ya."

"Okay. Fair enough. Should I, um—should I leave something for lunch?"

"Huh? No! Ya fuckin' nutball! Lunch was on me!"

The bell rang and a black kid named Sweetzer danced out and feinted with his left but not knowing it was a feint I lurched into his right. My head was raked round to a funny angle and

Sweetzer was working on my midriff. He landed a few before I jabbed him away, or maybe stepping back was his own idea because he immediately launched a hook that caught my right ear and set it ringing. He hit my head a couple more times and now everything seemed to be happening at a slight remove, as if they had switched over from the real fight to a meticulously realized but cottony reenactment. In it, I was tucking my head behind my forearms and dull concussive blows were falling upon my midriff and either side of my head. The stands were a booing darkness beyond the ring. The frowning referee danced to one side, angling for a view in past my looming foreground arms. Finally his striped shirt closed in and my opponent disappeared. My arms were pried down, and as the referee leered in, he held my gloved hands. I was grateful. They were heavy.

The referee's lips moved and a hollow voice boomed: "DO YOU KNOW WHAT DAY IT IS?"

I cocked my head at him. That this worried-looking man should interrupt the fight to scream banal questions at me seemed consistent with the bout's dreamlike turn. An answering voice rustled between my own ears: "Sure."

The booming voice said, "WHAT DAY IS IT?"

Fans screamed and sighed.

I could see the Sweetzer character now, in the background, dancing and shadowboxing in a far corner of the ring.

"Thursday," I heard the rustling voice say.

"DO YOU KNOW WHO I AM?"

"Sure."

"WHO AM I?"

A two-fingered whistle cut through the din. I looked around

for the fan who had given it. There were so many. I looked back at the ref.

"You're Frank Nardiello."

"OKAY. YOU FEEL OKAY?"

"Sure. You're Frank Nardiello."

He slapped my gloved hands together, stepped away, and swept a pointing hand at me.

Sweetzer rushed in and ducked under my jab. He popped into view close and something snapped my jaw back and I threw my arms out like an angel and balanced on my heels. I looked up, straight up. Somebody's mouthpiece was spinning away toward the light. It pinwheeled glinting droplets. The light was very bright. Around it, dark. Above was dark and light and light and dark, and gravity below.

"Boy, Joey, that last uppercut—*I* felt that one."

"Funny—I didn't."

"I would've throwed in the towel before then, but . . . it don't look so good, so early in the first round."

"I understand."

"Boy, Joey, you need to rest up a little."

"No no, I need another one right away."

"Kid, you know the boxing commission mandates a week between fights—"

"Irv, I don't have a week!"

"Hold your horses, Joey! *Three* weeks after a knockout."

"Three weeks!"

"Joey—"

"Irv, that's not gonna do it for me! This one was what, two-fifty? I need four hundred bucks, right now!"

"Or?"

"Or—" Or, I was going to say, I'd get the crap beaten out of me, but there was an obvious rejoinder to that. I didn't want to explain, though, that two beatings administered under the supervision of the State Boxing Commission were preferable to one beating administered under the supervision of Benny Benedeck. "I just need it," I said.

"Kid, lemme loan you one-fifty—"

"No, Irv, please." I knew that Irv lived hand to mouth like I did, and he was a sixty-year-old man. There had to be another way.

"Kid." Irv hesitated. "Joey. I'm not even sure I can get you two-fifty next time."

"I thought—what are you saying? I thought two-fifty was the bottom."

Irv looked at his hands. "I'm not sure I can get you another fight." He looked up at me. "Kid, it's the system. They don't like a guy who keeps getting knocked out in the first round. You know these animals in the stands. They want action, action, action. These're animals we're talking about, Joey—animals."

"I understand, Irv." Nice of him to blame the boxing fans for wanting to see some boxing. "Never mind. There's something else I can do."

There was nothing else I could do. I patted Irv on the back. But sometimes doing nothing is the best plan.

. . .

"Thanks for comin', kid. Take a look a this."

Benny had a down-at-the-heels office typical of the too-cheap-to-decorate old-world businessman, with a plastic slip on the sofa and battered olive metal filing cabinets and a pebbled-glass door that said BENEDECK IMPORTING. He had wheeled a TV and VCR on a castored cart into his private office and was loading in a tape. He was smiling as if somebody had flipped him onto his back and spent the last half hour gently rubbing his tummy.

"Mrs. Benedeck and me are now reconciled. I had this fuckin' brainwave, kid: I told her you'd been goin' to that motel for two weeks and I had so many goddamn pictures of her'n Lou Argo that if she thought she was gettin' a red fuckin' cent offa me she was outa her fuckin' mind. So we're gettin' along pretty good now, but you mentioning Muriel—Mrs. Argo—it started me thinking. . . ." He hit the play button. The VCR made a grinding nasal noise and after a beat the monitor showed a middle-aged woman and a young black man copulating on what seemed to be a cheap motel-room bed. Oddly, the tape's sound track included, in addition to the squeak of bedsprings, James Taylor plaintively singing "Fire and Rain." A dark, blurry shape covering the right quarter of the screen suggested that the camera was hidden by a drape or a hanging coat. A young white man stood to the left, next to the bed. He was watching the couple but was more or less ignored by them. He was also naked and was stroking his penis, which was erect.

"The dame is Muriel," Benny said placidly. He was watching the monitor with a faraway smile. "I know a bar she hangs out at, so's I hired these guys to go and make nice with her. You know, like they was picking her up."

The woman was tinnily crying out as the sex became more vigorous: "Do it to me, big boy! Do it to me, big boy! BIG boy! BIG boy! BIG boy!"

"Why James Taylor?" I said.

"Huh? The music?" Benny shrugged. "Somebody turned on a radio somewhere. Look, this is good."

The white man next to the bed was saying, "AAhhaahh-AAhhaahh . . ." He had an orgasm, soiling Mrs. Argo. She and the black man continued to copulate.

"So okay," said Benny, still watching the monitor. "You bring this cassette to Lou Argo and I'll forget about what you owe me. You take it to him, make sure he knows it's from me. That I seen it. And make sure you tell him, before he watches it—"

"BIG boy! BIG boy! BIG boy!"

"—make sure you tell him: The white guy is a Jew."

Lou Argo's office was much like Benny's except his pebbled-glass door made him out to be more of a polymath: LOU ARGO TRADING, INC. / ARGO REFUSE CORP. / ARGO PROPERTIES / LOU ARGO ASSOCIATES. A white-haired secretary was working an IBM Selectric typewriter behind a Formica counter.

"This is for Mr. Argo, from Mr. Benedeck."

She swiveled and took the tape from me. "Lou!"

A voice: "Yeah."

She got up and went through an open door behind her. I could see the corner of a wooden desk but not the man behind it. I heard her say, "From Benny Benedeck."

"Uh," went his voice. "Who brought it?"

"Some kid."

"Huh. Have him wait. Bring the thing in, will ya, Ginny?"

The secretary emerged. "Siddown," she told me. She wheeled a castored cart bearing an old TV and VCR, much like Benny's, into the back office. She emerged again, sat, and resumed typing.

Over the stuttering hum of her typewriter I could just hear "Fire and Rain," and shortly, "Big boy big boy BIG boy BIG boy . . ." I sat in a chair whose Leatherette upholstery was gathered into buttons that dug into my ass. It seemed like a long time.

The sound from the tape finally ran into a static hiss. There was the bleep of the monitor being turned off and, from Lou Argo's office, a long silence. The typewriter chattered on.

Lou's voice sounded: "Ginny."

"Yeah."

"Send him in."

Ginny looked at me. I rose, stiffly, and made my way around the counter. I entered Lou Argo's office.

Lou was sitting behind his desk in coat and tie, his pocked neck and jowls hanging over his collar. His nose was a spongy thing such as you might use to wash dishes. He was still staring at the dead monitor, even as he gestured at the chair in front of the desk and said to me, "Please."

I sat. At length Lou Argo looked at a wooden box on the desk in front of him, leaned forward, opened it, took out a cigar, trimmed it, lit it, took a puff, then held the cigar sideways over the desk and frowned at it.

"Tell me," he said. There was a long silence.

"Yes sir?"

He stared at the gently pluming cigar. "The white guy—was he a Jew?"

". . . I don't know, sir."

"Mm." He nodded. For the first time he looked at me. If he recognized me from the motel, it didn't show. "You see, dontcha, what's goin' on, between me and Benny Benedeck?" He took another puff on the cigar, then stared at it once again.

"Well." I cleared my throat. "Well, sir, it seems as if each of you is trying to establish dominance."

"Dominance?" This brought his eyes up from the cigar.

"Well, yes, sir. Through sexual, uh, it's not uncommon, in the animal kingdom—not that either party here is, uh—but you know, terrritorial markings, and the female, uh, well, male display, and uh—"

"Dominance . . ." He looked back at the cigar. After a musing silence he cleared his throat. "That sex act. Ya know, which you witnessed. Between myself and Mrs. Benedeck. You may a noticed I yelled the name a Benny Benedeck. Many times I called his name." He lapsed into silence.

"Yes sir," I said.

"In yelling his name. Does this mean I fantasize"—he waved his hand in a dreamy gesture—"about sex with Benny Benedeck? That I fuck, mentally, him? Does this mean that I am a fruit?" He gravely shook his head. "No—for I am not a fruit. No. What you have here, in this sex act, I piss in Benny Benedeck's ear."

"Yes sir, that's exactly—"

He was patting the air in front of him for silence. When the silence had run long enough, he resumed. "I piss in Benny Benedeck's ear. And Benny Benedeck"—he gestured toward the monitor—"pisses in my ear. This. This is what we have here."

"Yes sir. It's even interesting that you use the image of pissing in his ear, because of course that itself suggests—suggests—"

Lou Argo was staring at me. I shut up.

He drew on his cigar and said, at length, "There is bad blood between us. And therefore, these things. Which makes more bad blood. And then more things. You see what I'm saying?"

"I think so, sir."

"What a you think a this?"

"Well," I was encouraged by his interest, however intermittent. "Well . . . I'm not sure it's fair to the women."

Lou Argo scowled. He looked around the room, then back at his cigar, still frowning. Then he shrugged and gave me a frank look.

"So you see," he said. "I'm gonna have to have someone beat the livin' fuckin' shit out of you."

I swallowed. "Sir, I'm not sure I follow that last part."

"Well, you come in here, with a tape. My wife being fucked. By a nigger and a Jew. Well. Perhaps not *fucked* by a Jew. Please. Let's not split hairs."

"Yes sir."

"In addition, you regard myself in the act. And try to take pictures. Now these things, you will say, Mr. Argo, these were things at the behest of Benny Benedeck. Which is true. And of course he must pay for them as well. This does—"

"But, Mr. Argo, you yourself pointed out that that just leads to a vicious circle—"

"Please—"

"A never-ending cycle of pointless violence and—and—and mindless sexual activity and—"

"Please." He was again holding up his palms for silence. After a moment: "I did not say pointless. I did not say mindless. This is *your* view. Your opinion. The point is as follows. If one person walks in here, with a tape of my wife. Being fucked by a nigger and a Jew. And this person is not punished. Then the whole world will come in here, with such tapes." He drew on his cigar. After a long moment he shrugged. "These are the realities."

"But sir—but sir—may I suggest, if we just let it go, just this one time, I swear to you sir, I wouldn't tell anyone, so no one"—Lou Argo was nodding and smiling—"no one would know that anyone had, uh, gotten away with anything . . ."

He continued nodding. "This of course," he said, "is always the suggestion."

"But sir—"

"Made—"

"But sir—"

"Made—please!—with the sincerest intentions." He looked at his cigar, then inclined it to either side. "Word spreads."

"But sir—there's a particular reason, in my case—sir, may I explain?"

Lou Argo shrugged and turned up a palm as invitation.

"Well sir, you have to understand how I got here. I—I don't know how to put this—I'm not really *part* of this world at all. I just don't fit in, in a sense, so that these, uh, strictures, uh . . . Well sir. I was in college, you know, and when I got out of college I just, I couldn't bear to, uh, to just continue in this future that seemed to be set out for me. It would have been publishing maybe, or maybe advertising, or graduate school if I wanted to go into teaching, but—but—all of it seemed like death to me, sir. An office, a life like everyone else I knew, no surprises, no excitement, and I thought, why, what's the point, when I'm young and at liberty to choose anything. Anything, sir. The world is wide."

"Mm," Lou Argo murmured.

"So I chose something which I knew did have risks, and might hurt me, but I thought, bodily harm, well, if it doesn't kill me, well, then it passes, and I'll be a broader person, sir. Although I'm in the process of reevaluating that. But that was the idea. More a feeling than an idea, perhaps, sir. And perhaps not a good idea. But the point is I'm only here so as not to turn into one of those people in an office or university or advertising agency or what have you. I'm here, sir, more to learn and experience and grow and broaden myself. I'm not here because of socioeconomic pressures, sir. So accordingly I'm not really subject to the laws of, uh, the socio—uh, I don't know how to say this, sir. I'm—I'm on a safari. This is a safari, sir. I'm not one of the actual, er . . . animals, as it were. So the whole question of keeping discipline and so forth—you see how it doesn't really apply. How I stand apart, sir."

"Mm." Lou Argo was leaning back, his eyes closed. "So you're saying—let me understand this. You're saying, I can't beat the shit out of you because you're better than me."

"No! No sir! Well—yes—in a way—"

"Look. I think I can now sum up." He opened his eyes and eased himself forward. "Frankly, I say this. You speak from a core of confusion."

"But sir—"

This time he held up only one hand for silence. "Confusion. This life which you describe. Advertising. Teaching. What was it? Publishing. Nice offices. Air-conditioned, I'm sure. Carpeted. Furniture. The works. In the city, I pass the bars. Where these people drink. Nice bars. Is this a bad life? The clothes—nice. The offices—nice. The hours—not bad. After work, you go to a bar. Nice women go there. Girls who are also—in publishing. Clothes. Hair." He patted one hand near one ear, indicating stylish hair. "You pick one up. You fuck her. This is what these bars are for! You speak of different worlds: These girls, me they would not fuck. You, they will. One girl is not for you, you pick up another. You get tired of that, you fuck from behind. This you flee?"

"But sir—"

"Please! Open your eyes! See this! All that you have thrown away! The grass is always greener. The grass is always greener? The grass is *not* always greener. *There*, the grass is greener. You seek a different life. Superior in what sense? None. You don't see this. You express yourself—marvelously. However. It does not hide the inner core. Which is confusion. And so—you will have the shit beat out of you. Which is my last word."

"Why? Why? For God's sake! Always a beating! I don't understand it!"

"Well...kid...you've lost a couple fights, I don't know as—"

"I may be a *little* slower than the other guy, but not that much. I may be a *little* less strong, but I don't get beat by a little, Irv, I get the crap pounded out of me. Why is that?"

"Well, okay. Well . . . okay." He looked at me. "Should I tell you what *I* think?"

"Irv! Please!"

"Well Joey, it's like I've told ya: This fighting game, it's all mental."

"But then you said—"

"Huh?"

"Never mind. Yeah?"

"See, you gotta have this animal in ya. If you don't got that animal, see, it don't matter if you're fast. It don't matter if you're strong. Some guy who's an animal, he's always gonna beat the college professor, *even if that college professor is fast and strong*!"

"Right. Right."

"I mean you gotta, you gotta, kid, you just gotta," Irv's eyes narrowed and he bared his teeth and said, "AAAAAAAHHHHHHHH! I DON'T GIVE ONE FUCK ABOUT FAST AND STRONG! I'M GONNA TEAR YOUR FUCKIN' HEART OUT! AAAAAAAAAAAHHHHHHHH!" Irv glared for a moment. Then his lips slipped back over his teeth. He stood there panting. "Like anything in life, Joey, it's attitude. You can coach things that'll help. Little things. Sure. That's what I do—I help. But I can't give ya that attitude. You gotta have it. You gotta have it in ya to be an animal, and not a friggin' college professor."

"Do I, Irv? Do I have it in me?"

Irv gazed at me. He took too long answering, then realized he'd taken too long and gave a short embarrassed laugh.

I was walking home; a man stepped from the shadows.

"Joe Carmody?" he said.

THE OLD COUNTRY

He was ten years old when I knew him. He was a Hammer of God, defying not Rome or the crown, but the Hebrew school principal. His name was Michael Simkin. Like the great scourges of history—Genghis Khan, Oliver Cromwell, Omar Mukhtar—he seemed invulnerable, in his case perhaps because he was too young to execute. Or so we believed.

He had no program unless it were anarchy. The teacher would turn away from the class to face the blackboard; Michael would raise a circled index finger and thumb and through it push his other index finger, and rattle it around, ululating loudly. The teacher would whirl but never fast enough; at his desk Michael would be the picture of composure. Or, outside of class, Michael would direct the gesture at some weaker soul like Laurie Sellaway, a slight, innocent redhead who would reliably burst into tears, unaware perhaps that the sign represented sexual intercourse but nevertheless undone by its powerful vibe. Michael would shake his head and smile, marveling at her femmy lack of spine. "Bawling, Sellaway?" he would inquire. He came to adopt the dreamy manner of a monocled *Gruppenführer* with a pluming cigarette: "Bawlink, Tsellavaaaay?" he would murmur as she sobbed.

Or he would canter lopsidedly down the hall behind another classmate, baying like a jackass, eyes rolled back in his head as his right hand made a sweeping pantomime of jerking off. Or he would stage what in other contexts would look like coups of performance art. One day in the lavatory he peed on the radiator while loudly singing "O, Canada"; the stench of burning urine wafted through the school for the rest of the day. Another time he penetrated a cylinder lock securing a glass display case in the school's foyer. The case held black-and-white pictures mounted on posterboard, recording the history of the school's construction from freshly leveled lot to finished building, as if the modest two-story structure were an engineering feat on a par with the Brooklyn Bridge. The display ended with an incongruously smiling photo portrait (no one had seen him smile in life) of the principal, Rabbi Menachem Uvane. With Michael's stroke these pictures disappeared. When they were restored the next day a crudely drawn man squatted in the middle of the bulldozed lot, three circles dropping from his rear end to join a pile of such circles already on the ground. The same man—or perhaps his brother—now visited the building in each stage of its construction, leaving similar piles. And grinning Rabbi Uvane now had two small friends, one on either side of his head, each sticking a penis into his ear.

Michael was short, as Hammers of God go, and slight, and brown-haired, and slender-featured—almost ferret-faced. He had a large birthmark just below one cheekbone, advertising disorder. He wore twill pants of beige or light green; they would through inattention ride low on his hips and his button-down shirt would poof out at the waist. The lunch bucket he carried would rattle and bang against his thigh with each careless stride; he walked as if his shoes were too big, with a pigeon-toed shamble that set off the slovenliness of his dress. He was not self-conscious.

In Talmud Torah—"Torah Study"—Hebrew school—there was a snack bar that served as a holding area for the students before class. There Michael would sing his own version of the theme from *The Beverly Hillbillies*:

Let me tell ya story 'bout a man named Jed,
Took Ellie May and he threw her on the bed;
Down with the zipper, and up with the dress,
And into the hole went a bubblin' mess.

"We are the jolly bastards/of Lippman's AZA," he would sing, lampooning the anthem of the local chapter of the American Zionists Association. And along more biblical lines he had a song about five constipated patriarchs:

There were five, yes five,
Constipated men in the Bible,
Oh in the Bible.
The first, yes the first,
Constipated man was Cain:
He wasn't able.

And the second, yes the second,
Constipated man was Moses:
He took two tablets.
And the third, yes the third,
Constipated man was Balaam:
He couldn't move his ass.
And the fourth, yes the fourth,
Constipated man was Solomon:
He sat for forty years.
And the fifth, yes the fifth,
Constipated man was Samson:
He shook the house down.

We were dubious about Samson: Did "shaking the house down" really serve as a double entendre for constipation? There was much debate and Michael eventually changed the last verse to "David—he dropped a giant." But this seemed to suggest, if anything, the opposite of constipation. He changed it again to "David—Goliath couldn't make him drop," which had too many syllables. Our long debates about Scripture and scansion were cut short by the circumstances that ended Michael's singing forever—but more of that in its place.

In the snack bar cookies and juice were dispensed to the waiting students in order to pacify us. They were, in Michael's hands, amusements. He would take other children's cookies and lob them onto the tops of the vending machines at the back of the room. He would even throw his own cookies there. At the vending machines he would throw cups of fruit juice. He found a broom and opened new territories of food tossing by using it to push aside a piece of acoustical tile in the ceiling and then hooked cookies up into the hole. He then took to tossing copies of *Shiarim Hatorah*—"Gates of the Torah," our Hebrew school text—into the ceiling as well. He once threw another student's shoe up, and the teacher who climbed onto a stool to retrieve it also found, mysteriously to him, several copies of *Shiarim Hatorah*—an apparent miracle which, had it happened in Maccabean times, would have been the basis for a Jewish holiday. The teacher also found several tree certificates.

I should explain.

Michael Simkin's family was rich. This was common knowledge, in the way that it is among children. There was even a rumor, never substantiated, that the Simkins had a bowling alley in their basement, a rich-person's solitary lane with Brunswick pinsetting and belowground ball return. To us his parents' wealth was neither here nor there except during the tree drive. We were all encouraged to bring in money to be used to plant trees in the state of Israel, in support of her effort to make the desert bloom. For each tree endowed a student received a printed certificate bearing the signature of Levi Eshkol and the words " 'And when ye shall come into the land and ye shall plant . . . ' Leviticus 19:23." Michael had a dozen certificates, all of which he threw into the snack bar hall ceiling, and also a medallion for having planted ten or more trees, which he threw out the window of the Hebrew school bus at a pursuing dog.

Michael made a show of relief that his missing tree certificates had been found and thereby escaped punishment. When punishment was awarded, its highest form was to be sent to the office of Rabbi Uvane. Miscreants were usually escorted there by Slim, the goy who patrolled the hallways. Slim was tall, greatly tall, even by adult standards, and thin indeed, with a bristling buzz cut and a khaki jumper uniform. He had a grizzled hatchet face and beady eyes, and his head movements were quantized into short jerks so that, walking the halls and scanning from his great height for mischief-makers, he had the air of an old turkey buzzard cruising for rodents. He had on this occasion caught Michael socket-popping. This widespread diversion consisted of taking the foil from a piece of gum, folding it into a biprong tuning fork shape, using the gum's paper wrapper as insulator with which to hold the foil, and sticking it into a socket, which would then sizzle and pop as its fuse shorted out. Having caught Michael, Slim was marching him down the hall to Rabbi Uvane's office as Michael sang the following impromptu:

Down with butt-brain Uvane,
Down, down, down;
Down with butt-brain Uvane,
Down, down;
When you see Uvane
You feel butt pain
So down with butt-brain Uvane,
Down, down, down.

Slim walked impassively beside him, head jerking this way and that, ready to bag other infractors on the way.

Slim's position was the dehumanized one of useful outsider, like the non-Hindu hired to butcher dead cows. He was not only school disciplinarian, swifter afoot than the rabbis and therefore better equipped to catch hooligans, but also school maintenance man, called upon to make such minor physical repairs as Jews could not be expected to know how to perform. It was incongruous to hear the rabbis even pronounce his name—"Slim, could you take a look at the radiator in cheder eight, it's rattling like a son of a gun"; "What's the matter with this desk, Slim, the top won't come up"; "Slim, that light is flickering to beat the band." He would wordlessly perform the task, whatever it was, then go back to hall patrol, head jerking this way and that.

I remember him surveying the snack bar hall, arms folded, looking down over his beaked nose and the stiff spray of hair that bunched in each nostril, his mouth tightly hooked in its characteristic frown. Next to him stood Rabbi Ackerman in a blue serge suit, a full head shorter than Slim even measuring from the top of his stiffly steepled yarmulke. Rabbi Ackerman also wore a chiseled frown, and the two of them together looked like Mafia don and soldier; as they watched the children at play some sour understanding seemed to flow back and forth between the two. I'm surprised now that Slim had a rapport with anyone, but perhaps his oafishness was exaggerated by my own fears and prejudices. I saw him as a primal man whose head contained only instincts of predation and a knowledge of the use of hand tools. Or he was a throwback even to some prehuman age when cold-blooded creatures ruled the earth and pterodactyls thumped screeching through the sky.

Like a true henchman, Slim was variously useful; he also drove a bus. My bus, in fact. Talmud Torah met immediately after secular school, and its yellow buses picked us up from public school and shuttled us there. These same yellow buses would be idling out in the snowy lot when classes ended long after nightfall. Unlike the ride to Hebrew school, the ride home was not direct. Since the school serviced all of greater Minneapolis each bus carried students from quite a large area. The students were therefore sufficiently dispersed that they were let out not in bunches, but each at his door, and for those near the end of any given route the ride could be very long indeed. On my route I was second to last.

The bus would always start off noisy and full with Slim impassive at the wheel. Successive discharges and the soporific rumble of the warm bus would make it progressively quieter. Eventually all talk ceased and the vehicle trundled along in silence. Slim, lit by the dash, scowled through the windshield as the bus, an island of warmth, rattled across the planet's far side. Frigid starlight glinted outside, and inside we sat dazed, our stocking-capped heads bobbing with the motion of the vehicle. It was as if Slim were a reaper, mutely transporting the sad young damned to an unheated beyond.

Finally, finally, we would pull up before my home glowing in the snow. Slim would throw open the door, and I would rouse myself and fling myself out into the stinging cold. Waving my lunch bucket for balance, I would stagger through the massif of snow that the day's plowing had created between the street and our driveway. I would trudge up the drive and into the house, where the warmth would wash over me and instantly fog my glasses. Smells of dinner were part of the warmth. There would be two places set; as soon as I entered, my mother would start dishing up my dinner and her own. My father would be reading in the living room, having already eaten with my older sister, who would by now have vanished. I saw almost nothing of my sister from the onset of her puberty until she left for college six years later. She spent those years in the bathroom washing her hair. Very occasionally she emerged for food or to use the telephone, her head wrapped in a towel.

My mother would have finished spooning out the dinner by the time I put down my books and got out of my thick overclothes. The two of us would eat quietly, the only sounds being the clink of silver, the wind moaning outside, an occasional belch from my father in the living room, and from the bathroom the muted gurgle of water. When either I or my parents had to relieve ourselves in the evening we would go down to a dank and drafty half bath in the unfinished basement. I would always wear shoes because the cold harbored by the cement floor was sufficient, even through thick socks, to inhibit egestion. The pipes exposed overhead would dully rush and stop, hum and groan, as my sister in her warm bathroom upstairs fine-tuned the water temperature. Shivering, I would use the toilet and then hurry back up. Aside from being cold the basement always smelled of urine, not because of the bathroom but from the newspaper laid out for our dog, Tippy. Admirably enough, my parents considered it inhumane to put her out during the winter. Newspaper was therefore spread in the basement to serve as her toilet, but unfortunately all Tippy deduced from her paper training was that she was meant to urinate with her front legs on the newspaper, and therefore, depending on her orientation, she would sometimes pee onto the floor. When I cleaned up after the dog I would stuff the urine-soaked newspaper into a garbage bag—a brown paper grocery bag; plastic trash can liners were not then much used—with the soppingest part of the newspaper up, to lessen the chances of the urine seeping through the bag's bottom. I would then hurry the soft pungent bag through the door connecting the basement to the frigid garage and plunge it into a tin trash can, my breath making visible puffs in the bare bulblight. Back in the basement my gooseflesh would recede as I swabbed the wet floor with a mop that I would then leave standing in the slop sink. But the smell of urine, absorbed by the cement, lingered in the room. Even after the basement was "finished" and abstractly freckled linoleum was laid down, I imagined that the odor had been trapped underneath and that it had been absorbed as well by the pink insulation now covered by a paneling that ostensibly made the basement habitable.

One might say that the story of our family was composed of two eras: that in which we did not have a finished basement; that in which we did. The first era was marked by planning for and anticipation of the second. The transition, which took place when I was seven or eight, consisted of the installation of the linoleum and paneling; the covering of a high window, formerly bare, with an opaque oilcloth curtain printed with maps from the age of discovery with Latin place-names written across the misshapen continents and quaint monsters of the deep in the oceans between; and the addition, where there had been only studs, of an interior wall to separate the "living area" from a "laundry area" that retained its hopeless cement floor and cinder-block walls. After it was finished, though, the "living area" was still cold and oppressive, and we all avoided it. Whether my parents' plan to increase the house's living space by 50 percent was a crashing failure in their minds or only in fact, I do not know.

The finished basement's finishing touch was the purchase of a piano, and now, on Monday evenings, my dinner would be delayed even past Hebrew school by instruction upon it. On arriving home I would take off my coat and put on a heavy sweater as I said hello to Harold Marx, the itinerant piano teacher who was a member of our shul. Mr. Marx was a large man, and though the stairway had ample headroom through its top half, an upstairs closet encroached upon its bottom half, and Mr. Marx would have to incline his head as he led the way down. When I later looked at Diane Arbus's photographs they somehow reminded me of Mr. Marx, who subtly but disturbingly failed to fall in with our house's scale. Downstairs he would pull out the piano stool and we would sit side by side and perform songs like "As Those Caissons Go Rolling Along" and the theme from *Love Story*. After the lesson he would lead the way back upstairs and join my mother and me for dinner; he would praise my playing to my mother and the two of them would chat. I wonder if he knew I had a sister.

Mr. Marx's wife taught the clarinet. Like her husband, Lillian Marx wore thick glasses. She had an enormous ass and wore floral print dresses that billowed around oak-stump calves. I imagined that at home the two of them would rise each morning and wordlessly go to the music room, where Mr. Marx would sit at his piano and grind out a thumping boogie-woogie around which Mrs. Marx's clarinet would wrap swirling klezmerlike figures. Then they would segue into the theme from *Love Story*.

Then, sensing it was time for them to teach, they would rise. Each would grab a briefcase bulging with staff paper and climb into an aging foreign-made car to crisscross the town, hunched at the wheel and peering out at the snow swirling in the headlights. Work finished, they would return home, strip down to their eyeglasses, and put on pajamas which they would button to the neck. They would then climb into bed and stare at the ceiling until overcome by sleep.

Be that as it may, I detested the piano. I practiced only on weekends, during the day, because even finished, our basement was not well lit, and at night the cold and the smell and the hard sound of the piano in the low-ceilinged linoleum room were unbearably depressing. After two years of lessons I begged to be allowed to switch to the guitar so that I could practice upstairs.

By this time Tippy was getting old. She used to romp up and down the stairs two at a time, tail furiously wagging. But gradually her bounding thumpety-thump became a studied clack, clack, clack as she took the steps one by one. Where she had once exploded up out of the staircase into the kitchen, Tippy would now cautiously bump the door open with her nose, look around as if unacquainted with the room, spot a familiar face, and, as her tail slowly wagged, heavily lift each hind leg up out of the stairwell. She would make her way with a sagging hunch-shouldered walk toward whichever person was closest, her head bobbing in time with her slow steps. She would lay her warm muzzle in that person's lap and look up, waiting. For something. Her liquid brown eyes, always sweet, now grew mournful. Now, sometimes, I would hear her slow huffing progress on the stairs interrupted by the scrabbling of nails and a heavy thump as a hind leg gave out beneath her. And she would interrupt her naps in the living room to raise her head and howl, or look wildly about as if just roused from a nightmare. Finally Tippy could no longer manage the stairs at all and so, when she needed to relieve herself, would merely stick her nose out over the staircase and whinny. My father would carry her down and place her on the newspaper, where she would crouch and gaze at him sadly while her urine pattered.

Life went on: school, Hebrew school, the ride home with Slim, dinner. After dinner I would do some homework, perhaps watch an episode of *Judd for the Defense* or a television movie. One that I remember vividly was *Seven in Darkness*. For a week I had been looking forward to *Seven in Darkness*, having seen the previews. I ate dinner quickly so as not to miss the beginning of *Seven in Darkness*. When I settled in front of the television, end credits were rolling for the preceding show, and a voice-over announced the imminent start of a world premiere movie, *Seven in Darkness*. There were commercials, then another short preview showing a blind man bellowing in a booming thunderstorm as dramatic music thumped underneath. Rain, or perhaps tears, coursed down the man's cheeks. The announcer reiterated that the movie would be a world premiere. There was another manic burst of commercials and then a lingering silence, then a somberly intoned: "And now . . . *Seven in Darkness*."

The movie was about seven blind survivors of a wilderness plane crash. The sighted crew having been killed, the seven in darkness confronted the seemingly impossible task of finding their way back to civilization. Some of the seven in darkness despaired. But one of the seven proclaimed that though they were blind they were not helpless and that if they worked together they could survive. This man became leader. The seven in darkness groped their way through the wilderness, baked in the day's punishing sun, inched forward through the night's crashing rain, over mountain passes, through steaming swamps, hand in hand, single file, like elephants linked trunk to tail. After days of harrowing travel the original cowards renewed their counsels of despair. The leader, however, was resolute, and they proceeded on until the toe of the man first in line tapped cautiously onto macadam, and traffic whizzed by, and the seven in darkness were redeemed.

I was deeply moved by *Seven in Darkness*. For me the dark was connected to the turmoil of sleep. Sleep sometimes was easy. Sometimes, though, as I started to drift off, I felt myself floating back to the formless fears of early childhood. There was a certain way that the light from the hallway would fall across my cracked bedroom door, and the door's slanting shadow excited in me a dread that I could not name; it reached back to a time when I knew no names. I stared, and my heart would start pounding. I heard voices, but they formed no words, only tones. All of my senses fell away from each other, and the door and its shadow seemed not a part of any coherent world but only the mute outer form of my inner jumbled terror.

I describe all of this because of what happened to Michael Simkin. There was one, and only one, all-school assembly during my years in Talmud Torah. It was at the outbreak of the 1967 Six-Day War (though it was not called that at the time of the assembly—who knew?), and for want of an auditorium, it was held in the snack bar. We were called together so that the faculty could tell us about Israel's performance and prospects in the fighting just started. The main speaker was Ken Jacobson, an earnest teacher unlike most of the rabbis inasmuch as he was less than seventy years old, and who stockily strode the halls of the Talmud Torah in a cardigan sweater and knit yarmulke. (The old rabbis favored skullcaps of a slick black synthetic gathered into a hard button center.) Rabbi Jacobson straddled a chair and discussed the different fronts—against the Egyptians, against the Jordanians, against the Syrians; so many Arabs, so few Jews!—and reassured us that so far our young state of Israel was doing well. In the middle of the talk Michael Simkin, perhaps discombobulated by the fact that a classlike gathering was being held in the free zone of the snack bar, perhaps on a sugar high from having consumed that day's cookies instead of having heaved them into the ceiling, perhaps overcome with anxiety over the fate of his many trees now hostage to Arab aggression, but at any rate unable to contain himself, leapt to his feet and made the trilling sexual intercourse sign right at Rabbi Jacobson's face.

There was stunned silence. The rest of us forgot our petty concerns about our own trees and stared. So did the teacher. When Michael finished his finger rattling and sat, Rabbi Jacobson remained motionless for a long moment. Then he began to tremble. The trembling climbed his body. His face turned red. His hands levitated, vibrating, fingers bent like claws. Finally he erupted, roared, leapt up, hopped through the children sitting cross-legged on the floor. He reached down where Michael sat, grabbed a fistful of shirt, and yanked him to his feet. He hooked

Michael's armpit with his other hand so that Michael's shoulder rode up above his backwobbling head, and heaved forward. Michael's feet barely touched the ground as he was marched from the room.

Michael was not at school the next day. We eyed his empty desk. He was absent the following day as well. And the day after that. Finally, on the fourth day, Danny Alter raised his hand and asked Rabbi Davies if Michael Simkin would ever be coming back to resume his study of the Torah.

Rabbi Davies cleared his throat.

"That is up to his parents," he said. "And Rabbi Uvane."

A week later Michael did return, but it was immediately clear that something was wrong. In the snack bar he took his juice and cookies in silence and read from *Shiarim Hatorah.* When the bell rang for class he gathered his books and walked stiffly down the hall and into the classroom and to his desk, where he sat quietly, hands clasped in front of him, staring ahead, waiting for the teacher to arrive. During the class itself he raised his hand to volunteer for every question and, when called upon, always gave the correct answer. It was not just that he raised his hand, it was the way he raised it—arm held perfectly straight, thumb and fingers pressed together and curled to form an ice cream scoop shape, and with none of the desperate lunging and arm waving of the showboater or suck-ass. In the bus on the way home he also sat quietly, staring forward, hands clasped over the lunch bucket and books that were stacked neatly in his lap.

We tried to get a rise out of him, of course; we called him Bonsche the Silent and Brainiac and the Golem, but he did not respond; nor did he respond when we waved a hand before his eyes as he sat staring at his desk, nor when we shoved or rabbit-punched him or pulled his hair. Eventually we gave up. For the next several months Michael was a model student, if somewhat robotic, until his family moved to California, where (it was common knowledge) all meshuggenehs end up.

This is a true story. Of course it now strikes me as terrible that a ten-year-old boy was destroyed by parents who were tired of managing him. But it also strikes me that at the time it gave neither me nor his other classmates pause. We saw no tragedy. We ourselves were acquainted with a terror deeper even than that which Michael's parents had visited upon him through beating or some other form of what we would now call abuse. Fear was a fact of our own lives, and so we did not sentimentalize it. In fact we were happy enough to shove Michael around ourselves. For the other children as for me, neither Michael's situation nor any other event at school or at play was as compelling as one's own bedtime. Everything I saw and did during the waking day was a distraction; it was in bed, waiting for sleep, that I confronted the world directly.

When my parents had people over I would be put to bed early. My father would have come home with a couple of heavy clinking bags from Smyrdyk's, the discount liquor store. He would shave, my mother would change, and I would be tucked in to lie listening to muffled clunks and rustles of preparation. A sudden distant ring of the doorbell would send footsteps tapping away to end in the musical coo, dulled by intervening walls, of my mother making greetings at the front door. A long interval and then the bell would ring again, and then again, more and more frequently, each time followed by greetings, the thunk of the door shutting, and heavier footsteps approaching as my father brought new coats to pile onto the bed in the bedroom next door. These footsteps receded, the voices in the living room swelled, and the party was under way.

I would sometimes be bold enough to climb from my bed, push the door open, and walk down the hall toward the chatter of adults. When I got to the living room I would stand peeking from behind my father's chair, which was closest to the hall, and blink against the light, one hand clutching the chair's carved wooden back. Someone would notice me; guests would beam and say, "Who's that? Who's behind Daddy's chair?" I never told them, for two reasons. One, I wasn't there in order to socialize. Two, they knew perfectly well who I was. My parents would let me stand and listen for a few minutes, and then my mother would usher me back to bed.

As I lay there once again, listening to the voices from the living room, the quiet of my own mind began to yield to the *tohu vavohu* of Genesis. The voices would become a murmur as the sense of the words dropped away. They were a texture, like the smell of cigars and cigarettes that they floated in on. Louder noise—laughter—would poke out suddenly and then subside. And then it would all slip away.

When the world came back the house was dark and the voices gone. It would take a moment for the horror of that fact to sink in. The quiet was a thing very different from the cocktail party, and I could not yet comfort myself with the assumption that the world had persisted between the two. The world was only what was in front of me, and it was now hard with silence. My stomach would begin to leap. The voices had been a warm thing that I could flow out toward on my way into sleep, but this silence was a great wall hemming me in. Eventually a deep rhythmic chanting would develop inside the silence. My closed bedroom door, and the walls too, developed greater and greater force in their stillness as if bearing up under increasing pressure, like the hull of a sinking ship. It was the pressure of silence, silence, the world's worth of silence, all focused on me. I could not face it down; I had no words to push it to arm's length, and my screams crashing against it made not a dent.

I never met Michael Simkin's parents, though I have a vivid false memory of his father standing on the lot upon which their house is to be built. His hands are on his hips and a pith helmet shades his eyes; he is directing the operations of a backhoe as it digs a trench for the ball return. Though I remember it now, years later, it is something I could have imagined only then. In the beginning there was fear, a deep shadow that goes with the gaudy colors of early youth. It shades Michael's father's face as he stands unmoved while around him heavy machinery roars and the earth trembles; it makes a monster of Slim the Talmud Torah goy; it dwells in the narrow creaking staircase of our own little home. Some forget that darkness, and the silence, and the chaos inside. But despite what Scripture says, it will never be banished, for without it there would be no horror, no misery, and no childhood.

COSA MINAPOLIDAN

On a bleak December day in 1965 two men in topcoats elbowed their way past the counterman and into the back office of Esperanza's Pizza. One of the men was chunky and thick-boned, his shoulders pushing at the seams of his overcoat. He had ginger hair and a broad open face and was young—early twenties, perhaps. The other man was older, dark, thin, Latin, wearing beneath his coat a dark suit and a white shirt and a thin black tie. The two men faced the owner of the pizzeria, Arturo Esperanza, across his small cluttered desk.

The redheaded man, standing slightly ahead of the dark man, shuffled his feet, looked down at the floor and then, with effort, forced himself to look Esperanza in the eye. He swallowed, looked back at the dark man, and, when the dark man nodded, looked back at Esperanza.

"Joe de Louie don't like waiting," he said. "You've kept Joe de Louie waiting since Wednesday. He ain't used to it and he, ya know . . . he don't plan to start getting used to it . . ."

The redheaded man fell silent, still staring at Esperanza. The dark man leaned up to him and said quietly:

"Call him a name."

"—Fuckface," said the redheaded man, and blushed.

Esperanza stared at them. The eyes of the redheaded man wavered. The dark man was attentive, watchful. Esperanza, who was slight and owlish, sighed. "Mr. de Louie knows I been having problems. I don't wanna stiff Mr. de Louie—hell, I'd have to be crazy. I pay, always pay, and this time just like always, but I need a little time—goddamn you bet! See for yourself what it's like out front!"

The redheaded man looked dumbly at Esperanza, who thought that maybe he'd put across his point. Out front the pizzeria was indeed empty.

The redheaded man shifted. Pips of sweat had sprung out on his forehead. For long seconds there was only the distant sound of traffic. Finally the dark man leaned up to him and said, "Does Joe de Louie care about this guy's problems?"

"—Joe de Louie don't care about your problems. He's a businessman, not a complaints department. It's his money and—and he wants it. . . . He's not a complaints department." The redheaded man ran his tongue over his lips. "—Fuck-face."

Esperanza said, "Whatever I got belongs to Mr. de Louie, but right this minute I ain't got nothing. Go look in—"

The dark man interrupted, talking to the redheaded man: "Sock him one and ask him what he thinks about it."

"Ahh!"

"What do you think about it?"

Esperanza reached up to rub his eye. The dark man was again speaking to the redheaded man: "Now tell him."

The redheaded man said, "Have the money by tomorrow, or you'll find out what." He started to turn, paused for a moment, and then did turn, and walked out.

Before following him the dark man shrugged at Esperanza. "He's new."

There was a history. Joe de Louie had been born Luigi Castellano in Naples in 1915. He was an orphan—his father had died in the Great War, his mother was carried off by cholera soon after—and was officially the ward of an elderly aunt. But in fact he was a child of the streets. This did not harden him as it did other children orphaned by war and disease. Though he learned to beg and steal, and did so without conscience, neither did he swagger. For him it was a way of life, not a form of rebellion, and even as a teen he had a cheerful equanimity that made him easy to like.

At the age of sixteen, tending to stockiness and already starting to bald, Luigi Castellano moved to New York, sent for by a cousin. There he called himself Louie Castles, but he never became comfortable with the English language. At twenty-two he moved to Cleveland, still running with an outlaw crowd. Fancying himself a ladies' man, he started calling himself Lou Adonis. When a howling drunk who claimed to be a friend of Joe Adonis's broke Luigi's right leg with a crowbar—"as a warning to yas"—he started calling himself Joe de Louie. He toyed frequently with the idea of changing his name again, but didn't change it again.

De Louie spun his wheels in Cleveland for many years. His name rarely came up in discussions among the Cleveland bigs, and when it did, he was not marked as a comer:

"Who's de Louie?"

"He's a fat kid, a bald kid, a fat bald kid."

"Yeah, he's a fat—they call him Joey Dome."

"No, Joey Dome, he's lanky. He's onna South Side, runs with that putz Lou Nickles."

"At's *Johnny* Dome."

"Johnny Dome. Right. But it ain't de Louie."

"So who's this guy I'm thinking of? Who's this asshole . . ."

"Maybe it's, uh . . ."

"You sure it's not de Louie?"

"It *is* de Louie—I'm saying, who *is* de Louie?"

"Is he thinking, you remember, there was this guy . . ."

These were the years of stagnation. Finally, in 1962, at his weekly card game with a crew that was by now largely younger than him, de Louie broached the subject of a new start:

"We move, eh?"

"Yeah, okay, Joe."

"Where we move, Joe?"

"I tink maybe we move"—his eyes darted around the table—"Minapolis!"

"Yeah, okay, Joe."

"How come Minneapolis, Joe?"

"You see." Joe nodded vigorously. "Is good, Minapolis. Is good. You see."

"Yeah, Joe, okay."

It was an odd choice, Minneapolis. To be sure, it was virgin turf; its Swedes, Poles, and German Lutherans had never organized on the model of eastern towns. But there seemed little to organize. The city had not much serious crime. It was dotted with scenic lakes. The people were polite. Many owned boats. In the summer they engaged in water sports; in the winter they skied. The stolid northern stock seemed immune to the great miseries and grand passions upon which crime traditionally feeds.

De Louie's real reason for choosing this particular spot was, like the true motive behind many a grand plan, surprisingly slight. Joe de Louie thought that "Minneapolis" was Chippewa for "New Naples," and he missed his native Napoli. He assumed that Minneapolis would resemble it, with its lakes somehow standing in for the lagoon, and with other similarities to be discovered by moving there. When he did move there, and learned better, his disappointment was tempered by the sheer pleasantness of the place and, besides, they were ready to kill Knutson.

He was chosen, Knutson was, more or less at random. The de Louie mob had been in town for several weeks with nothing accomplished, and it was felt that they should kill someone in order to establish their bona fides. De Louie and his top lieutenant, Dominico Cacci, therefore wanted to make the execution very public, and Knutson's shoe store, for he was a shoe merchant, had a plate glass front on Hennepin Avenue. It was felt, however, that the assassins should not be drawn from the de Louie mob itself, whose inexperience might tell, and whose fledgling members might be unduly discouraged if their maiden erasure should happen to go bad. Accordingly two outside pros, Kenny Boils and Maurizio "Mimi" Chicago, were called in special. De Louie decided to throw them a party the night before the hit.

The arrival of Boils and especially of Mimi Chicago, who had a rep, caused quite a stir in the de Louie organization. At the party the men approached Chicago with the hesitant friendliness of mediocre ballplayers greeting a newly signed ace.

"Hiya, Mimi, Joe Rossi here."

Chicago grunted.

"Hiya, Mimi; Mike Vitale. How's Chi?"

"How do I know how's Chi? I'm from Philly; Chicago's my name fuck an idiot."

"How are ya, Mimi; Joey Scaggs."

Chicago grunted.

"Yay, Mimi, Tony Grazzo. How's things?"

"How do I know how's things; Chicago's my name fuck an idiot."

The party was counted a great success in spite of the fact that Chicago clearly detested everyone he met, and that the neglected Boils spent the evening in a sulk. At any rate the next day Chicago and Boils gunned down Knutson without incident, if such may be said, and left town.

. . .

"Iowan alla you whores should workiffa me."

The whores—this was some days after Knutson—didn't know what to make of it. At five feet three inches de Louie was not, on first sight, a commanding figure. His face barely showed over the lectern, its few long strands of hair combed over a round and otherwise bald head. He reminded some of the ladies of Baby Huey, but they were impressed by his suit, which was manifestly of fine quality, and they recognized in the little gentleman a certain old-world charm, though they wouldn't have known to call it that.

The circumstances of this convocation had been not alarming exactly but certainly odd. The ladies had been pulled off the streets by awkwardly deferential Italians in dark suits and carted across town in a fleet of windowless vans. Now the ladies, thirty of them or so, were seated on folding chairs in a dusty meeting hall. At the back of the hall was a long folding table covered by a linen cloth marked by faint yellow stains, upon which were set out a coffee urn, cups and saucers, and untasted cannoli. In front, Joe de Louie was stepping down after his brief remarks, and his slender, hawklike lieutenant, Dominico Cacci, was taking the floor.

"Mr. de Louie he don't speak English too hot so I'll fill you chippies in onna details. From now on we take half a what you make. No bitchin', 'cause I know lots a you girls been givin' your pimps more. And we give you somethin' them pimps never did: You get arrested, you give us a call, we get you sprung. If any your boyfriends don't like the new arrangement, just refer 'em to me. My name is Dominico Cacci."

"He's cute. What he say his name was?"

"Minnie Go-Gotch."

"Minnie's a funny friggin' name for a guy."

"I don't care. He's cute."

Cacci *was* darkly handsome, though his mouth would sometimes hang open. Up on the podium, he cleared his throat. "And if any you girls got ideas about not payin' up, just remember Knutson." Like everyone else in the de Louie organization, Cacci pronounced the name Nutson. He turned to step down, but turned back with an afterthought: "And from now on yas work onna buddy system."

"He sure dresses nice."

"He got style. What he say his name was?"

The girls were loaded back into the vans and returned to the streets. To those who recalled the evening later it would seem an hallucination with no cause and no consequence, for they never heard from the Italians again. The reasons for that were bound up with Knutson, whose name, even correctly pronounced, none of the girls had ever heard.

The hit had never gotten the play that the organization had hoped for. Their assumption had been that an assault by topcoated gunmen would signal gangsterdom's arrival, bringing screaming headlines and making the protection rackets viable. But Chicago and Boils had, reasonably enough, waited until the shoe store was empty before charging in for the execution, and since no one saw the assailants, the police, reasonable in their turn, had looked for killers with a motive. It developed that Knutson had a wife, and Knutson's wife a lover named Erickson, and that the only alibi for each of them on the afternoon in question was the other. Furthermore, Knutson carried, not unlike many prosperous businessmen, a fair amount of life insurance benefiting his wife. The eleven bullets dug out of Knutson, having come from two different guns, were explainable on the hypothesis of a love pact between the adulterous Swedes, who had presumably emptied their guns in a sex-heated frenzy. The overkill, to the authorities, betokened passion, not professionalism.

When a grand jury indicted the two unfortunate Lutherans, Joe de Louie found himself in a delicate position. He wanted to exculpate the pair without of course incriminating the free-lancing Chicago and Boils. He hit upon what struck him as a romantic solution: He would himself provide the widow with an alibi. But when he came forward with the claim that "Mrs. Nutson, she spend the afternoon wit' me," he was met with skepticism, and not only because he couldn't pronounce the woman's last name and didn't know her first. An outraged Mrs. Knutson herself denied the story, and the upshot was that she and Mr. Erickson were ultimately acquitted of the murder, since no evidence but only opportunity could be laid at their door, and Joe de Louie was convicted of perjury.

"O Goddan," he said, when his verdict was handed down. His criminal record was a serious black eye; he was given two years in the state penitentiary at Stillwater. "Hey, mout'piece," he said, upon receiving sentence, "wadda do bow dis?"

But the sad fact was that the mob was powerless to help its capo. On the eve of his surrender they threw him a party which held bittersweet echoes of the Chicago-Boils affair.

"See ya, boss."

"Yeah."

"So long, boss. Chin up."

"Tanks."

"It'll be over before you know it, boss."

"Yeah. Sominabitch bas'."

With Joe de Louie in the big house, the organization drifted into decline. The Sioux and Chippewa Indians who lived on Minneapolis's south side would stare dumbly at the swarthy Mediterraneans who spoke cryptically of whores, numbers, and Nutson. Any Italian who ventured onto the Polish turf of Northeast Minneapolis simply got beaten up. The mob was reduced to preying on the city's minuscule Italian community, and that not very effectively. The mob had never really found its feet, and the redheaded Irish youngster who terrorized Esperanza the *pizzaiole* was typical of the class of muscle they were recruiting.

But the mob would soon be galvanized by news from Stillwater.

"Hear about the big fella? He got his troat slashed by a homo."

In an atmosphere where status attached to having inside

information, but where there was little of real consequence to talk about, the rumor spread quickly, was greatly embroidered upon, and was universally believed to be fact. The story, by the time it finished making the rounds, was going something like this:

In the prison showers Joe de Louie had rebuffed the homosexual advances of a man convicted of soliciting sex from a state trooper. The frustrated homo had repeated his overtures on the exercise yard during a game of artillery ball. He had again been rebuffed. Smarting, the homo had stolen a spoon from the mess and had spent two months honing one edge down against the wall of his cell. Just as he had arrived at a serviceable weapon, it was discovered and confiscated in a prisonwide shakedown. The persevering homo had stolen another spoon, spent another two months honing it, and had then used it on the throat of the by now unsuspecting de Louie.

"Hear about the big fella? He got his troat slashed by a homo."

The truth of the matter was that Joe de Louie was alive and well in Stillwater, patiently serving out his term. He had been neither the victim of any assault nor the object of any homosexual amours. But the members of his organization disliked prisons and never visited, nor did de Louie expect them to, so that he did not miss them once the story gained currency, and never suspected that his mob thought him dead. He continued in his daily routine, shuffling to mess every day, his prison-issue trousers hitched high on his squat barrel torso, greeting other cons with a short jerky wave of the arm and a murmured "Heh!" or "Hayeh!"

"Hear about the big fella? He got his troat slashed by a homo."

Dominico Cacci convened the organization to discuss the situation.

"We gotta do sumpn," he said.

One of the men nodded. "We draw straws. Loser gets himself troad in jail. As soon as he finds out which homo did it—" He drew a finger across his throat.

Cacci shook his head. "Suppose they don't send him to that prison?"

"Could ask for a transfuh."

"Yeah, and suppose he don't get it? Look, killin' just exactly that particular homo, that don't bring the big fella back to life. That particular homo, he ain't important. It could a been any homo."

"So . . . we gotta kill just any homo?"

Cacci nodded. "That's how it looks from here."

"Well if we kill just any homo it don't even gotta *be* a homo. I mean, can't nobody tell once he's dead."

This provoked a heated discussion about whether it was possible to tell from a dead body whether its tenant had been a homosexual. Many maintained that it was. "Homo zaygot itty peckers. *Così*," said one thug, crooking a little finger.

"How would you know, Raf?"

"Common knowledge."

"Among homos."

There was jeering and laughter.

"All right, knock it off," said Cacci. "For the big fella, we make sure."

But killing a homo in Minneapolis in 1963 was easier said than done. No doubt they existed, but they had no public gathering places, or at any rate none known to the de Louie organization. It was suggested that the organization "go underground," but what exactly this meant no one could say. There was much nervously subdued discussion until Cacci finally proposed that they get the more cosmopolitan Cleveland organization to send them a homo. He had a contact who, for the right price, would deliver anything. Greatly relieved, the de Louie organization approved the idea.

Cacci rang Cleveland from a public telephone and outlined the problem, holding a handkerchief over the phone. Cleveland indicated that they would kill a homo immediately and send him right up. Cacci cut in that he didn't want to pay for a hit but for a live homo, since the point was for Minneapolis to wreak the revenge. Cleveland replied that if money was the concern, they would in fact charge less for a hit, since live delivery entailed all of the same difficulties, plus those attendant to kidnapping. Cacci grumbled. Cleveland, feeling give, declared that live delivery was impractical and, in response to further grumbling, said that they would not deliver live for any price. Sadly, Cacci gave in. There was some haggling over money, and finally Cleveland guaranteed a dead homo in Minneapolis by the following evening.

The next afternoon the members of the de Louie organization started drifting into the service station garage that was the appointed site of delivery. They were all there by six-thirty when a white Pontiac Bonneville with blackwalls pulled up to the garage door, gave two short honks, and was admitted.

Its driver climbed out and looked from face to face. His eyes rested on the interim capo's.

"Cacci?"

"Yeah."

"Gianni Barca. Your stiff is inna trunk."

He popped it and stood back.

Inside was a middle-aged man in tan slacks and a sport shirt, packed in dry ice. The organization crowded around. Though they wouldn't have admitted it, most of them had never seen a dead man outside of a funeral parlor. A couple of them, following Cacci's example, squeezed and palpated like sensible shoppers. They seemed satisfied. Cacci, however, was frowning.

"He's been dead a week, this guy; he's not fresh."

"Well he's been in my trunk alla way from Cleveland." Barca shrugged. "I don't think he looks so bad, considering."

"No, he looks real good. Peaceful. That's why I say. You sure he didn't die of natural causes?"

"Waddaya talking natural causes, pull up his shirt. There's the bullet hole, see there?"

Cacci inspected the chest wound. ". . . He bleed much?"

"Bleed? Buckets he bled. We cleaned him up after."

"Dummy. We *want* blood."

Barca shrugged again. "I'm a mind reader."

". . . Jeez, it's all clean." Cacci was fingering the shirt. "What did you, change his shirt after? You changed a stiff's shirt?"

"That's right." Several mobsters recoiled in disgust. "Bought him a new one, thought you wanted it first class." Barca smiled thinly. "My mistake."

"Mm." Cacci pulled the shirt back down. He looked for a moment. ". . . So how come there's a bullet hole in this new shirt?"

Barca looked. "Goddamn . . . I guess they didn't buy him a new shirt after all. Cheap bastids. I told 'em to, thought you wanted it first class."

Cacci was still frowning. "So this is the shirt he was wearing when you clipped him."

"Yeah, right, there's the bullet hole."

"But there's no blood on this shirt, around the bullet hole."

"Yeah, that's right, I told 'em to wash it."

"You told 'em to buy a new shirt and wash this one?"

"No no, I told 'em—lemme think back a minute here—I guess I told 'em, Look, after you shoot this fairy, buy him a new shirt, or at least wash his old one—"

"We called you yestiday—"

"—I mean make him look all nice and nice. So I guess they just washed it—"

"We called you yestiday—"

"—thief bastids, I gave 'em money for a new one, seven dollahs I gave they said they used—"

"Yestiday we called and he's been dead a week this stiff; he's not fresh."

"Naw, he's just hard there from the dry ice."

"Mm . . ." Cacci was rubbing a thoughtful finger around the bullet hole in the shirt. He looked at the finger and abruptly slapped Barca on the back of the head.

"Wha?"

"They wash his shirt and the blood comes off?"

"Right?"

"But the powder don't?"

Barca quickly surveyed the surrounding faces. They were crowding less around the body now, more around him. He swallowed. ". . . I'll tell you the truth. I don't know what the hell they did with his shirt. His shirt, I don't know what the story is, I gotta delegate responsibility don't I?" He shook his head. "All I know, yesterday morning this guy's a screaming fairy." He chuckled. "Then boom!"

"You tell me that?" Cacci stepped closer, glaring. "I am a fully made guy ten years here and you ask me to believe this guy ain't been dead a week? Let me tell *you* what happened. You *bought* this guy from a mortician, maybe stole him even, didn't even pay cash. Then you shoot him inna chest, you pack him in dry ice, you cart him up here and you ask me to believe he ain't been dead a week." He slowly waggled one finger. "This is not good. This is not respect."

Barca doggedly shook his head. "All I know is, yesterday morning this guy is sucking cocks like a madman."

"We don't pay for this."

"What!"

"We don't pay for this."

"Then I take him back. I know where I can get cash for him."

"You don't touch him, you."

They chased Barca off, slit the dead man's throat, and late that night drove to St. Paul and dumped him on the steps of the capitol building with a note pinned to his chest: FOR THE BIG FELLOW.

. . .

"The homo thing," as they came to call it, turned out to be the de Louie organization's last hurrah. For a while it gave them something to talk about, Mimi Chicago and the subsequent "legal shit" having long since been talked to death. But the homo discussions too became more hollow. The spiritual erosion that had begun with de Louie's imprisonment continued. To be sure, Dominico Cacci was liked and trusted, but he lacked de Louie's charisma; he was Aaron merely to the Moses who had led them to this promised land. Now people began to drift away, mostly eastward—back to Chicago, Cleveland, and beyond to the East Coast. Those who were left were not surprised when a story began to circulate: "Hear about Cacci? He's bein' brought in onna big deal inna Bahamas." Cacci himself commented only with significant silence. Soon he did indeed disappear, in his colleagues' minds as the story's consummation; in reality, to work at his brother-in-law's beauty parlor supply business in Newark. More mobsters drifted away. Those who stayed put down legitimate roots, a few even taking jobs with the Italian businesses they had formerly terrorized.

When Joe de Louie was released from prison in 1965, his mob had disappeared. He who had never complained accepted this too without complaint, but he did sometimes wonder. One day, walking down Marquette, he ran into Giorgio Coccovizzo, whom they had all called Coconuts, and who was now working as a steamfitter.

"Hey, Coconuts!"

"Heya, boss."

"Hey, Coconuts," said de Louie, throwing a stumpy arm into the air, "wha happen?"

"Well," explained Coccovizzo, "we thought you was dead."

De Louie stared at him for a long moment, and then nodded. "Heh!" he said.

He used his meager prison savings to open a two-chair barbershop on the fringe of downtown. He put a sign in the window: NO HIPPIES. He had a few steady customers, mostly elderly. Business was not good. In 1967 he took down NO HIPPIES and put up a new sign: UNISEX HAIRSTYLES. It fooled no one, and business remained slow.

On the afternoon of September 12, 1968, Pete Peterson, a retired mail carrier, came in for his biweekly trim. De Louie was slumped in one of the barber chairs, a copy of *Field and Stream* lying open on his stomach.

"Yay, Joe, Humphrey gonna beat that son of a buck Nixon, wuddya think? . . . Joe?"

Joe de Louie was buried in a pauper's grave. The barbershop was garnisheed for delinquency in property tax and two years later was torn down to make way for a new bank.

HECTOR BERLIOZ, PRIVATE INVESTIGATOR

VOICE: My name is Berlioz. I'm a private dick.

The first three notes of *Symphonie Fantastique* chime.

Their ring-out leaves behind the distant echoing tap of high heels climbing in a stairwell.

BERLIOZ: My office is on Franklin up in Hollywoodland on the eighth floor of a building that would scare away the carriage trade if I drew any. The halls are dirty and the elevator is usually on the fritz, but some folks manage to find their way up: dopes, schmoes, weepers, whiners, souses, hopheads, and the occasional stuffed shirt. I suppose they're all God's children; I wonder if He's touchy about it.

The high heels, having grown steadily louder, leave the stairs and approach along a hallway.

BERLIOZ: I'd seen it all, or thought I had. Then one day—September 14, 1947—*she* walked in. Since then, I *have* seen it all.

A door opens, tinkling a shopkeeper's bell.

BERLIOZ: Or think I have.

WOMAN: (breathing heavily) Berlioz Investigations?

BERLIOZ: (in the scene, not narrating) It says so on the pebbled glass.

WOMAN: And who are you?

BERLIOZ: You *do* need a detective.

WOMAN: Not Berlioz, surely?

BERLIOZ: Berlioz, Hector. Go ahead and park it; I know it's a long walk up.

A chair scrapes.

WOMAN: No receptionist? No associates?

BERLIOZ: I have a temp in when there's heavy gunplay. Well, you figured out *my* name; how about putting us square?

WOMAN: Dolores O'Doole.

BERLIOZ: How may I help you—*Miss* O'Doole?

DOLORES: Yes. Well. My situation is dire, Mr. Berlioz. I'm recently bereaved; my father died two weeks ago.

BERLIOZ: My sympathies, Miss O'Doole.

DOLORES: Thank you. But Dada (she stresses the second syllable: duhDAH) had been ailing, and in pain; the end, when it did come, was almost a relief.

BERLIOZ: (barking) So I was out of line with that sympathies crack, is that your point?

DOLORES: Why—why no, I—

BERLIOZ: Then suppose you stick to your story!

DOLORES: Yes—yes, of course, I . . . He was—he died, as I say, two weeks ago. There is a will, in the hands of his lawyer, a Mr. Emeric Geneen. Geneen is a large, bluff, blustery man; I've never cared for him. When he called to inform me of the terms of the will, I was surprised to learn that—

BERLIOZ: (quietly) I apologize, Miss O'Doole; I guess I popped my cork.

DOLORES: Oh. No, that's quite all right.

BERLIOZ: Nice of you to say. Please, go ahead.

DOLORES: Very well. Mr. Geneen informed me that Dada had left everything to the Campostello Foundation. When my mother died several years ago, Dada established the foundation to do research into Campostello's Pox—that's what she died of.

BERLIOZ: My sympathies, Miss O'Doole.

DOLORES: Actually, she'd—Thank you. At any rate, Dada was a wealthy man and has left the foundation magnificently endowed. I myself have no money. That would be neither here nor there were I certain that those were indeed Dada's wishes—and were the foundation honestly run. But its director is a crony of Geneen's, a Pole named Szmyrninski. He is not a man of medicine. He is—well, I can't know what he is, but he strikes one as a gangster. Smooth, charming even, but a gangster.

BERLIOZ: So your concern is that your father's will is less than valid; that Geneen either manipulated him or falsified the will itself; and that your father's foundation is being run as a milk cow for Szmyrninski and Geneen.

DOLORES: Just so, Mr. Berlioz. May I smoke?

BERLIOZ: You can do handstands for all I care. What's Geneen's address?

A match is struck.

DOLORES: The Leander Building, on State Street.

BERLIOZ: Uh-huh. You mentioned certain financial woes; how do you propose to pay me?

DOLORES: I have friends, resources; I didn't mean to suggest I was indigent.

BERLIOZ: Surely not. All right, Miss O'Doole, I'll put my best man on it.

DOLORES: (she titters) . . . Heavy gunplay. You're quite amusing, Mr. Berlioz.

BERLIOZ: You should hear my Georgie Jessel.

The opening three notes of *Symphonie Fantastique* chime out.

WOMAN: May I help you?

BERLIOZ: Hector Berlioz to see Mr. Geneen.

WOMAN: Do you have an appointment?

BERLIOZ: Tell him it's regarding the Campostello Foundation. My card.

A telephone handset is uncradled.

WOMAN: Mr. Geneen, there's a Mr. Burly Ox to see you concerning—

BERLIOZ: *Berlioz.* Eck-dor *Berlioz.*

WOMAN: —a Mr. Egg Door Barely Oakes to see you regarding the Campostello Foundation . . . Yes . . . Yes, Mr. Geneen.

The phone is cradled.

WOMAN: Go right in, Mr. Barrel Ease—

BERLIOZ: Thank you.

A door is opened.

GENEEN: Mr. Beerswiller?

BERLIOZ: Berlioz.

GENEEN: Yes. Emeric Geneen. Have a seat.

BERLIOZ: Thank you.

Leather creaks, very loudly.

GENEEN: Interesting name.

BERLIOZ: French.

GENEEN: Wonderful people, the French. Beautiful women, fine wines, and of course . . . the windmills.

Leather creaks, loudly.

BERLIOZ: Yes.

GENEEN: I knew a Frenchman once. Fellow named Le Clare, though he spelled it Le Clerk. Died of typhus. I did his estate work. Had to fill out a bunch of French forms. Pain in the neck, but I guess they know what they're doing.

BERLIOZ: I guess.

GENEEN: Now, Campostello. Excellent organization. They do fine work. What's the nature of your interest in it?

Leather creaks, loudly.

BERLIOZ: I'm a friend—*was* a friend—of Gottfried O'Doole's.

GENEEN: My sympathies.

BERLIOZ: Thank you. But of course Gottfried had long been ill, and in pain; I felt it almost a relief when he died.

GENEEN: I see your point.

BERLIOZ: You're a cool customer, Geneen. At any rate, when I heard about Gottfried's foundation I thought I might contribute to it, in lieu of flowers, as it were. In lieu of a *lot* of flowers, if you catch my drift.

GENEEN: That sounds very generous.

Leather creaks, loudly.

BERLIOZ: That's the kind of schmengus I am. But before I fork over, I'd like to learn a little about the setup. I thought you, as Gottfried's lawyer, might be able to put me wise.

GENEEN: Surely. Campostello endows research into the cause of Campostello's Pox; we hope to contribute to that body of knowledge from which someday a cure will be derived. To that end we make research awards to doctors and institutions.

BERLIOZ: Who decides who gets these awards?

GENEEN: The foundation is run by a fellow named Leon Szmyrninski.

A low, admiring whistle.

BERLIOZ: That's quite a handle. He's a doctor, this Polonaise gent?

GENEEN: Lee—his friends, and I consider myself one, call him Lee—has been many things in his day but no, physician has not been among them. He was a seminarian in Crakow in the thirties, but fled before the kraut tide. Here in Los Angeles he runs an institute for spiritual betterment called Upsilon. That's a Greek letter; it means *U* and stands for, uh . . . upsilon.

BERLIOZ: Mm. Pardon my schnoz, but how much gravy gets skimmed?

GENEEN: I'm afraid I—

BERLIOZ: What kind of salary does he pull down, Szmyrninski, for running the foundation?

GENEEN: Oh! None; he works gratis, as does the rest of the board—that's me, the secretary, and John Frawley, our treasurer. He was Gottfried's accountant.

BERLIOZ: Sounds clubby.

GENEEN: I suppose. But only those close to Gottfried and Hortense would devote the kind of time and energy the foundation demands, without seeking recompense.

BERLIOZ: There's a point. Maybe you could put me on to Szmyrninski so's I can give him the once over.

GENEEN: Surely.

A switch is hit.

GENEEN: Lorraine, please give Mr.—please give our friend here Lee Szmyrninski's address and telephone on his way out.

Leather creaks as Berlioz rises.

BERLIOZ: Thanks for all the help, Geneen. Hope I didn't leave any sweat marks on the chair.

The three notes from *Symphonie Fantastique.*

We hear a door opening and the tinkle of the shopkeeper's bell.

BERLIOZ: Come on in, Miss O'Doole. If you've come for a progress report, I'm afraid as yet there isn't much.

DOLORES: Thank you, Mr. Berlioz. I just happened to be in the neighborhood, so—

We hear the pthoonk! of a bottle being uncorked.

BERLIOZ: Buy you a drink?

We hear pouring glugs.

DOLORES: Thank you, it's a bit early for me.

The glugs continue.

BERLIOZ: It's ten-thirty.

DOLORES: Mm.

The glugs continue.

BERLIOZ: In the evening.

DOLORES: (blandly) Yes, well, you know what they say.

The glugs finally stop. We hear Berlioz take a sip.

BERLIOZ: (hoarsely) I suppose.

DOLORES: Did you see Geneen?

BERLIOZ: I saw him. Didn't find him to be large, bluff, or blustery. Pretty smooth, as far as that goes—though what he doesn't know about France you could almost crowd into the Rose Bowl.

DOLORES: Did you confront him on the will?

BERLIOZ: What will?

DOLORES: Father's—

BERLIOZ: Oh! Oh, that, no, I didn't feel like getting into a whole big thing. You're a very striking woman. Is it natural, the blond?

DOLORES: Yes. Yes, it is.

We hear another loud sip.

BERLIOZ: (hoarsely) And the shape is yours, there'd be no disguising that.

DOLORES: Yes.

BERLIOZ: It's just that, in my line, things aren't always what they seem.

DOLORES: You're attractive yourself. I like men with red hair. Shocking red hair.

BERLIOZ: Call me Hector.

DOLORES: I didn't call you Berlioz.

BERLIOZ: Mm, but call me Hector.

DOLORES: Hector. Hector.

BERLIOZ: I'd like to mash my lips against yours. How would that be.

DOLORES: Yes, Hector. Yes.

BERLIOZ: Yeah. Yeah, I guess I will at that.

We hear a hasty sip being taken from the drink, then the unmistakable impact of lips.

The three notes of *Symphonie Fantastique* chime out.

A rapid-fire exchange:

CHEERY WOMAN: Upsilon!

BERLIOZ: Gesundheit.

WOMAN: Beg pardon?

BERLIOZ: Old gag. Szmyrninski in?

WOMAN: Whom shall I say?

BERLIOZ: Berlioz.

WOMAN: Gesundheit.

BERLIOZ: Touché.

WOMAN: Beg pardon?

A door is opened and shut.

VOICE: (mellow Polish accent) Mr. Berlioz?

BERLIOZ: Yes. Mr. Szmyrninski?

SZMYRNINSKI: Have a seat, please.

BERLIOZ: Thank you for seeing me.

SZMYRNINSKI: Not at all. I'm always eager to discuss Campostello. Emeric Geneen told me the reason for your interest; what can I add to what Rick has undoubtedly told you?

BERLIOZ: I'd like a list of doctors and hospitals that have received your grants.

SZMYRNINSKI: To what end?

BERLIOZ: Just to make sure you're on the up-and-up. I'm the kind of shmegegge likes to run the white glove over a dingus before he buys.

SZMYRNINSKI: Indeed. But how do I know that *you're* on the up-and-up, Mr. Berlioz?

BERLIOZ: How's that?

SZMYRNINSKI: (pleasant throughout) Well, how do I know that you really are a prospective donor rather than, oh, for instance, an all but insolvent private detective?

BERLIOZ: I pay my bills.

SZMYRNINSKI: Really, Mr. Berlioz.

BERLIOZ: All right, so I'm a shamus—what's it to you, Szmyrninski? Do you have something to hide?

SZMYRNINSKI: Poppycock. Why should I deal truthfully with those who would not deal truthfully with me? The door, Mr. Berlioz, is behind you.

We hear Berlioz rise.

BERLIOZ: All right, palski, here's how it stands: I'm friendly with the boys down at bunko. Let me know by the end of today whether you'd prefer to talk to me—or them.

The three notes from *Symphonie Fantastique*.

A phone rings.

BERLIOZ: Berlioz Investigations.

VOICE THROUGH PHONE: Hecky, it's Feeb.

BERLIOZ: Yeah, thanks for getting back. They check out?

VOICE: Them research grants? Beats me. But Szmyrninski did—fer poimanent!

Musical sting.

BERLIOZ: (narrating) Feeb Feeny was a friend in the bunko division. He had the charm of a Carthaginian and the brains of Piltdown Man, whom he resembled, but on the force I'd saved his life once when we were busting up a circle jerk in Koreatown, so I could turn to him for the odd favor.

FEEB: So you call us, tell us this guy's a crook, and he shows up dead.

BERLIOZ: Any suspects?

FEEB: Go look in the mirra.

BERLIOZ: Don't be a chump, Feeb. I wouldn't steer the bulls to a guy I'd just shown across.

FEEB: You might, Hecky. You might if you was subtle.

BERLIOZ: What the hell is that supposed to mean?

FEEB: A classy thinka.

BERLIOZ: I know the word, Webster, but why would I put the cops on to my own victim?

FEEB: T'row us off the scent.

BERLIOZ: Sure, the old I'd-never-do-it-so-I-must-a-done-it gag.

FEEB: That's it. Subtle.

BERLIOZ: Remind me: How'd I bump him?

FEEB: Blunt inscreminsk. Sappo, y'ask me; it ain't recovered. Nor the Polack neitha! Ha-ha! Ha-ha-ha-ha-ha!

BERLIOZ: (narrating) Feeb, though psychotic, was a good man. He vouched for me and the police let me go with the traditional don't-leave-town et cetera. But there was a surprise waiting for me back at the office.

DOLORES: (surprised) Hector!

BERLIOZ: What're you doing here?

DOLORES: Why . . . nothing, Hector—I—

BERLIOZ: What're you hiding behind your back?

DOLORES: Hiding? Why, nothing, I—Hector!

We hear her being grabbed; paper rustles.

DOLORES: Hector, these papers—what are they?

BERLIOZ: Why were you looking through my drawers?

DOLORES: Hector, it was perfectly innocent, I assure you! I was waiting for you, thought I'd take you up—belatedly—on the whiskey you offered—

BERLIOZ: At ten-thirty?

DOLORES: Last night, yes.

BERLIOZ: This morning.

DOLORES: You offered—

BERLIOZ: Last night, yes. But you decided to drink it at ten-thirty this morning?

DOLORES: I've had a bad night, Hector, drinking heavily—after your kind offer I left, but decided to drink heavily, elsewhere; this morning I woke up—headache, trembling, hair of the dog—drove to your office, the door was open, remembered your kind offer, rooted frantically for a drink, and found this—paper. This strange paper. With groups of lines—

BERLIOZ: Staff paper.

DOLORES: Yes. With notation on it. Musical notes. Melodies written out—for different instruments?

BERLIOZ: That's right, doll. A score. So I write music. Symphonic. Romantic. Using all the colors of the orchestra—what of it?

DOLORES: Why, nothing, Hector, I—

BERLIOZ: Now that you know *my* dirty little secret, let's hear yours.

DOLORES: Whatever do you mean, Hector?

BERLIOZ: And quit calling me Hector. Why didn't you tell me Szmyrninski was your uncle?

DOLORES: He was my *uncle*?

BERLIOZ: So you know he's dead.

DOLORES: No, I mean—he *was* my uncle?

BERLIOZ: So you knew he was your *uncle*.

DOLORES: I had no idea. But then father never talked about his rel—

BERLIOZ: Your mother. Her maiden name—Szmyrninski.

DOLORES: Yes. I see—it seems so obvious now.

BERLIOZ: You thought I'd throw a scare into him, but it didn't work. He had control of your father's estate and planned to keep it—

DOLORES: He was a greedy man. Smooth, charming even, but a gree—

BERLIOZ: And so you killed him. Grabbing whatever happened to be at hand—a bookend, a poker, a bust of Themistocles—

DOLORES: No! The rest is true. And it's true that we quarreled! But he was alive last night when I left him! In fact he was on the phone, to—Geneen!

The three notes of *Symphonie Fantastique*.

SECRETARY: You can't go in there, Mr. Barley Oats! He's studying some briefs!

A door is flung open.

BERLIOZ: Drop your briefs, Geneen! We have to talk!

GENEEN: See here now! What's the meaning of th—

BERLIOZ: Your colleague is dead!

GENEEN: Who the devil are you talking about, Berkowitz?

BERLIOZ: *Berlioz.*

GENEEN: Never heard of him.

BERLIOZ: *I'm* Berlioz.

GENEEN: You look fine to me.

BERLIOZ: I *am* fine. Your *colleague* is dead.

GENEEN: If you're referring to Lee Szmyrninski, he was hardly my colleague, though we were close.

BERLIOZ: So you *know* he's dead!

GENEEN: Don't be an ass, man; it's been in the papers.

BERLIOZ: . . . Don't think I won't check!

GENEEN: For pity's sake, Bergstrasser, if you must stay, don't stand there bellowing like a banshee!

After a short considering beat we hear the slap and creak of leather.

GENEEN: (irritated) . . . Yes, we were close, Lee and I, which is why I told Dolores I couldn't help her.

Leather creaks.

BERLIOZ: Dolores?

GENEEN: O'Doole, my niece.

Leather creaks, louder.

BERLIOZ: Your *niece*?

GENEEN: My sister is her mother's brother's wife.

BERLIOZ: So you're Gottfried O'Doole's—

GENEEN: Brother-in-law, yes. And also Lee Szmyrninski's, which is why I could hardly defend her for killing him—

BERLIOZ: She asked you to?

GENEEN: She called just now, before you trampled in. Sounded like she'd been drinking, heavily; apparently she's being placed under arrest. But defending her would put me in a serious conflict position, so I told her—say!

Leather creaks, footsteps recede at a trot, and a door is flung open.

GENEEN: Where are you—say! Bartók!

We hear the three notes of *Symphonie Fantastique*.

We hear faint echoing steps climbing a stairwell at a weary trot. As they grow closer they slow and scuffle. Finally they stagger down the hall and a door is thrown open close by, tinkling the shopkeeper's bell. We hear panting as the footsteps stumble across the room, and then the squeak of upholstery and castors as someone plops heavily into a desk chair, still panting. A phone is uncradled and a number dialed.

VOICE THROUGH PHONE: Police central pre—

BERLIOZ: Bunko!

We hear filtered switches and connections as Berlioz continues to pant.

ANOTHER VOICE THROUGH PHONE: Feeny.

BERLIOZ: Feeb!

FEENY: Yeah, Hecky, I thought I'd get a yowl from you. Yeah, we pinched her—

BERLIOZ: You're a chump, Feeb; she no more did it than you or I.

FEENY: Except *our* prints wasn't on the paperweight we found—wit' da Polackses' blood on it.

BERLIOZ: So? She'd probably been in that office a dozen times, handled the paperweight, and—

FEENY: It was in her purse.

BERLIOZ: Well, she might've needed it for—

FEENY: And her skin was under his fingernails, where he'd tried to claw her away.

BERLIOZ: It may've—

FEENY: And he'd managed to write her name on the floor in his own blood before he went croakski.

BERLIOZ: Are you sure it—

FEENY: And her address: Dolores O'Doole, 59654 Santa Monica Boulevard, Apartment Three-C.

BERLIOZ: Did you—

FEENY: Los Angeles.

BERLIOZ: So, so far it's circumstantial.

FEENY: Hecky . . . she confessed.

BERLIOZ: . . . And you believed her.

FEENY: Sorry, Heck. I can see you was sweet on her.

BERLIOZ: You're making a big mistake, buster! You—

We hear a disconnect and dial tone.

After a beat Berlioz's phone is cradled.

A sigh.

There is the trundle of a desk drawer being opened, the rustle of loose papers being pushed aside and the clunk of something heavy being taken from the drawer.

There is the pthoonk! of a bottle being uncorked, followed by pouring glugs.

The glugs last a long time.

They stop and there is the squeak of the bottle being recorked.

A sip is taken.

The chair creaks and we hear the click of a dial followed by the whining fade-in of a radio broadcast. It is a ball game. There is not much action; the play-by-play man announces balls and strikes over the susurrous background of a listless crowd.

BERLIOZ: (narrating) All right, the case might not seem like a corker to you. But I've never since met a woman who's affected me like that. So every night still, come ten-thirty time . . .

We hear the desk drawer opening, the clink of another glass being taken out, the pthoonk! of the bottle being uncorked, and many, many pouring glugs.

BERLIOZ: . . . I pour an extra one for Dolores, on the monte player's chance that she'll come back through that door and take me up on that drink we never shared.

The glugs finally stop and there is the squeak of the bottle being recorked.

BERLIOZ: . . . And, as if she's there with me, I make a little toast . . .

Another sigh.

BERLIOZ: (in the scene, murmuring) Here's to ya, sweets.

Glasses clink. The one on the desk thuds over and we hear its liquid piddling onto the carpet. Berlioz gasps and grunts a "woops" under his breath. The chair castors squeak and his footsteps pad across the carpet.

BERLIOZ: (narrating) I know. It's a dream. Maybe even a silly one.

We hear the ratchet and tearing sound of a paper towel being pulled from a dispenser.

BERLIOZ: But in this sad-eyed circus fat lady of a world of ours, maybe it's the dreams that keep us going—the cockeyed lies we tell each other—the stardust balm we spread on our wounded souls.

Footsteps cross the room again.

BERLIOZ: So every night, 'round ten-thirty time, I pour one for Dolores . . .

His knees crack as he squats, grunting, and pats the paper over the spill on the carpet.

BERLIOZ: . . . and every morning as well.

The three notes from *Symphonie Fantastique*.

ANNOUNCER: Tune in next week for *Bedrich Smetana: Oral Surgeon*.

Gong effect.

FINIS

HAVE YOU EVER BEEN TO ELECTRIC LADYLAND

I don't know. I do not know. A sick fuck. A sick, twisted motherfuck, that much is obvious.

An individual name does not come to mind. I'm not saying it was a stranger. Though it *could* be. Senseless, random. Or *not* random. A stranger, but not random. Because, officer, if you have, like me, a certain renown, name in the papers, well—I don't have to tell you that there are nuts out there. You know that better than anyone. A lot of nuts. And this, clearly—this is nut's work.

But more likely it was someone I know. It seems like such a personal thing. A statement, almost. I'm sure in the mind of this sick fuck, he was saying something. Possibilities? Officer, you don't get where I am without creating resentment in certain quarters. People without talent, sometimes it is incumbent on me to inform them. And they don't say, Well, he's right, I *am* a sorry piece of shit. Or the person who has been bested in a business transaction, they don't tell themselves, Well, he fucked me in the ass fair and square. No no, it's, He's a liar, he's a cheat, he promised me X, promised me Y, Z, whatever. You know what I'm saying. It can't be *me*; it must be *him*. It *sounded* like a good deal. There *is* a Santa Claus. And then, yes, disenchanted, they could lash out.

Well yes, I could list the possibilities. I could list—in confidence, right? I mean, these are people I have business dealings with, so, I mean, when you interview these people it won't be, uh, that *I* suggested that they might've, uh—and what *is* the crime, technically? I mean, breaking and entering I assume, since they had to do that in order to do the, uh—but what *is* the crime? What would they be charged with? Some kind of, uh, willful, uh, abuse of—

Right. You just gather the information. And then the district attorney's office, uh . . . So you're like the A&R guy, man. You're out there doing it. Then the district attorney's office—the guys in the suits—decide what to call it. But you're out there doing it, man. Fuck the suits, man. Like me. Ha-ha-ha. But I wasn't always a suit, officer. I used to be A&R. In the old days we—huh? Artists and Repertoire. You know, we would go out, sign guys, find the hot new bands, give them guidance. A&R, those are the guys who are plugged in. Like you. And then report to the schmucks in the suits. Like me, now. Ha-ha-ha. Don't let this hair fool you, man; I've turned into one of the fucking suits. I'm the *top* suit, man—ha-ha-ha! Can you believe that shit? We *are* the fucking shore patrol, man—ha-ha-ha!

Right, the possibilities. Okay. Frankly, I would make number one on your list my fucking cunt wife. Live here? In this house? Are you fucking kidding me? Whoa! Don't scare me like that—

ha-ha-ha! Whoa, shit—BOO! Ha-ha. No, she lives in the hills. And I don't know the fucking address. I do not spend time there, believe me. I do not dwell in the House of Cunt. Never been to the place. Yeah, separated. Cynthia. Yeah, same last name. God help me. Yeah, right at the top of your fucking list of suspects. Why? Why do you think. Resentment. Of a personal nature. Look, I—I don't want to put Cynthia down. I love Cynthia. There are things between us, years of struggle, heartache, joy. But she is a fucking cunt.

Do you want some wine? Glass of wine? Oh, right—on duty, right. I get ya. Let me just get myself—this thing has really got me—Constancia? Glass of wine, please? Blanco? Thanks. Well, Cynthia could still be feeling, you know—the woman scorned. Harboring that thing. *Will* not let it go. That would be the reason there. And it seems this thing—obviously, there is a sexual thing here. I mean *you* tell *me* what it looks like. But you don't have to be Sigmund Fucking Freud to see a sexual thing in this thing.

Or maybe not. Maybe just hostility. But I think it could be related to Delhi. No, *h*-i. Like in India, not like the corner deli. Delhi is my girlfriend. And I'm just saying, in Cynthia's mind, perhaps she's saying something about me and Delhi.

Or, it might have *been* Delhi. Delhi might have done it. This is unlikely; she's a very sweet girl. But not impossible. You want all the possibilities, right? Delhi, not impossible. Delhi Lund. Very nice girl. But look, she's young, sometimes I feel almost like a parent. And I establish limits. I have a lot of money, but I don't have *all* the money, you know. I leave a little for the other guy—ha-ha-ha! I don't have *all* the fuckin' money. So sometimes I have to say no. Like the man says, You can't have everything—where would you keep it? Ha-ha-ha! But that's what I mean. Limits. I tell her, No, Delhi, you cannot have, whatever, you cannot, you know, the bounds of reason. Limits. So occasionally, strife. But unlikely. Low on your list. Way down the list. I mean, she loves that dog almost as much as I do. Very unlikely. Not impossible. Very unlikely. Delhi Lund.

And then of course business associates. Various. There's Nathan Silver. Head of Monsoon. I signed one of his acts, the Hasta La Huega Sunshine Band, back in the eighties. Well, by then it was his *only* act. That was pretty much the end of Monsoon, uh—Silver's fallen on hard times. He lives in the Marina now. Jesus. And he probably thinks I induced Hasta La Huega to leave him. But these guys were over twenty-one! They're gonna do what they do! And I mean, they were shopping! I mean I know for a fact that Ron Rapke over at Intercourse was talking to 'em. And Silver says no, Rapke was only talking to 'em about doing a track on the Screamin' Lee Wintercort tribute album. Which is bullshit. I mean maybe he was, but you think they didn't talk about other shit? Ron *Rapke*? Come on. Matter of fact he should go on the list too. Ron Rapke. When the Japs were talking about buying his company last year some guy from *Billboard* calls and asks me for a comment, would Jap ownership change anything, I said I dunno, did they change Nanking? Ha-ha-ha—it was the fucking lead in the story, Ron's stock dropped four points. But my point about Nathan is, he's sitting in his little fucking condo in the Marina, brooding, doing what, who the fuck knows, producing Ronco dollar records, whatever, and he's probably very fucking angry with me. Very fucking angry. But this is the business we're in. The fact is, officer, everyone is in play, always. But Nathan wouldn't see it that way. He would take it personally because he was my rabbi coming in. He brought me up in this business. Great guy. Good times. This was back when he had a little label, Veronica. Singer-songwriters, some fusion acts. Nathan gave me, oh, let's see, Cost Report, the Paul Somer Concordance, that kind of thing. Fruity stuff, but quality. This was the seventies, when you could sell that shit. This was when I was A&R. That's right. Artists and Repertoire. Good times. Good times.

Actually I started in personal management. My roommate in college was Kenny Ramen. That's right, Ramen & Bogardus. The Ray Man. Shit, we had some fun. You know, we started, he was just a coffeehouse act, right out of college I started handling his shit, booking him in the Cambridge area. He was kind of the local legend, man. Which meant he got to fuck whoever he wanted. And then we went national. And *I* got to fuck whoever *I* wanted.

Now? Oh shit, he's not doing anything now. He started worshiping that guru, fuck, what's his name. Amdor something. Amdor Saachi-Wannabe. Something. Shit, what the hell is it. Yeah, and Kenny changed his name to Farhad something or other, wears a towel on his head and smiles all the time. Weird smile. Like his underwear binds. I am the One, or maybe I got jock itch, one or the other. Haven't seen him in years. Fucking guy moved to Jihad, I think. Is that a city? Sits there in his fucking tent all day contemplating his herd of camels. I guess this would be suburban Jihad. Outlying Jihad. Greater fucking Jihad. Although I hear he takes his jet to Frankfurt twice a year to get his teeth cleaned. Poor Kenny. Talk about disappearing up your own asshole. Me and Don Bogardus used to laugh about it. Well, *I* used to laugh about it, Don is kind of a tight-ass.

I mean I know Kenny's thought process. After *Traveler* came out he had all the fucking money in the world, and all the fucking *pussy* in the world, you know, more pussy than Jesus. *And* the apostles. And he figures, Whoa, wait a minute, pussy on demand and I'm still not absolutely positively perfectly fucking happy—what the fuck is going on? I thought that was *it*, man. So where do I get the whole thing, the orchestra seat, man, the absolutely-positively-perfectly-fucking unimpeded seat on the contented fucking aisle? Where do I sign up for *that* happy horseshit? And if you're not too bright—and believe me, officer, Kenny Ramen is a dear guy but no A. F. Einstein—then you start listening to these sharp son of a fuckheads selling tickets to the absolutely-positively-perfectly-fucking happy what have you. And bango, next thing you know you're sitting in some shithole country where they don't let you drink alcohol and the girls smell like home fries.

So I don't think Kenny would've done this. Because, finally, he's too fucking dumb. And I know, I know, you're thinking how smart do you gotta be to do this, this, uh, this thing, but I'm saying he's in one of those happy religions where they would frown on this. Yes, they bug people in airports, but that's the worst they do. And even there, it's the lower-echelon bugging people. Kenny is level Smegma-Seven or something. *He* doesn't have to dance in the fucking airports. Believe me, these religions, it's not like they don't give out the backstage pass. The superstar pass. Everybody does, are you kidding. With six fucking Grammies, are you kidding. And the platinum and the double platinum and the triple platinum. *Traveler*? Are you fucking kidding me? They go, Thank you, Kenny, or Farhad, or whatever the fuck you want us to call you, don't worry about bugging people in airports, we'll just give your finger cymbals to some other poor schmuck and you just hand over your money and you can go sit and watch your camels hump each other. Thank you very much.

Huh? DCT? Why do you ask about him? Oh, you read about that, huh? Man, that's going back. Yeah, this was when I was still in management, but I also had my own label, Valhalla. So fucking Dennis Christian Turner sues me for conflict of interest. He's saying I can't manage him and sell his records. Well, let me give you my reaction to that. Bull. Shit. That conflict of interest made Dennis Christian Turner a multi-fucking-millionaire. I don't bear him any grudge, though. Hey, it's business, he wanted out of his contract, so he fucked me out of it. I respect that. *And* the publishing. Jesus, I fucking *owned* Dennis Christian Turner. Valuable stuff. A very talented singer-songwriter. Sensitive stuff. He's gay. Not that—I mean, hey, gay is fine—are you gay? No no, no reason, I didn't mean anything, I just mean anyone could be. Relax, officer. I'm saying it's not that DCT is gay, which is fine, different strokes, it's not the gay; he's way beyond gay. *Way* beyond. He's, you know, his boyfriends'll come over—I know this, this is industry fact—they'll come over and he has this glass-topped coffee table. And he watches, he lies underneath, and the boyfriend'll squat on the table. Yeah. Squat on the table and take a dump. And Dennis Christian Turner is under there, whacking off. Very talented, but he's—

You have to understand, officer, these guys, they move to L.A. and hit it big and all of a sudden there's no more rules. They don't have the interior values to guide them. And the exterior rules, the social rules, they no longer apply. Not to stars. So whango—off they go. Nothing to stop 'em. Like when you unpinch a balloon—whee!—shooting all the hell over the place. No stability. No brakes. No nothing. They go out and do a little coke. And nobody says stop. So they do a *lot* of coke. And nobody says stop. So they buy a trash car. And nobody says stop. So they buy a reinforced glass coffee table. Or a herd of fucking camels.

See, you need strength of character. Which, in modesty, I have. You know, I'm not out there, I'm not a balloon out there, whiz whiz whiz, disappearing up my own asshole. You know. I have the strength of character to run a public, uh, you know, there's a board of directors I have to report to. So in that sense there are rules. But these artists—Jesus.

She's a fan of his, huh? So you *are* married. Well, don't tell her then. Let the man just be his music. I mean I like Dennis Christian Turner too. But always, there's the artist, and then there's the man, you see what I'm saying. Yeah, best not to tell her. Let her stay in that groove.

Yeah, I guess he should go on the list. Because he thinks I fucked him. "Conflict of interest." And he thinks he fucked me back with that lawsuit, but he's wrong about that. Nobody fucks me back. He did me a fucking favor. That lawsuit made me get out of management. Personal management, that's no business, man. Sweat your balls off, and then you gotta give the artist eighty-five percent. No, man, you gotta intercept the revenue stream earlier, you know what I'm saying, officer? That's what made me concentrate on the label. DCT made me what I am, in a way. Fucking dicklicker. Yes, he should be on the list. Fucking asshole.

Speaking of looking for happiness, you should put Darryl Downs on your list. You know who he is. Well you know, he married the woman who was giving him his enemas. Unbelievable. Colonic irrigation, they call it. It's a goddamn enema. Talk about unpinching a balloon, it turns your asshole into a goddamn soda siphon. Fucking Old Faithful. Stand back, she's gonna blow. You know, the earth starts shaking and people look around and scream and dive for cover. Germans and Japs with their little families grinning and taking pictures. Not really, I'm just saying. And Darryl Downs is a guy, married eighteen years, wife, two daughters, some chick starts giving him enemas and he sees God. He dumps his family. And his music—this is when he starts playing the smooth jazz. You know Darryl Downs's shit used to be funky, but this woman starts sticking nozzles up his ass and all of a sudden he hears smooth jazz. You explain it to me. Anyway, he looks like he's happy, like Kenny Ramen, but in fact Darryl is a bitter fucking man. Last year as a gag I send his younger daughter, on her bat mitzvah—his first wife was Jewish, looked like a goddamn horse, I used to call her Mrs. Ed—last year I send the daughter an enema bag. "On the occasion of your Bat Mitzvah," a little note on it, "so you'll know the way to a man's heart." A gag, right? Well you should've seen Darryl go off on me at the reception. Really. I was embarrassed for the guy. Haven't spoken to him since. Yeah, this is a bitter fucking guy. Don't let that flowing blond hair fool you. This is a deeply unhappy man. This would fit the profile.

Then there's Marty Symond. You know, the singer. Voice, not so great. Like an alto shofar. Ha-ha, like a—that's a ram's horn. It's used on—ah, forget it. Anyway, punk rock. He sings. Maybe you know him as Gene Damage? And the Flippers? No? When they broke up he was front man for The Burl Ives Explosion. Two albums with us. Then he broke up with his girlfriend, Liddy—Liddy Mitz—she was in the band—I say girlfriend but you gotta wonder, always strung out, it's hard to imagine erections and tits and so forth between those two—anyway, they broke up and she formed Crotchrot, and now he sings with Faster You Fuckers. If you can call it singing. These people don't know that punk is over. I had to tell him. I said, Marty, you can fix your teeth now. He still doesn't believe it. When we dropped him from the label he told me he was gonna skullfuck me. I said, Okay, Marty, just bathe first. These fucking guys. He doesn't have a record deal now. You can see him at the clubs, if you stay up late enough. Yeah, you know, this could be Marty. He could've done this. On a straight day, you know, if he could figure out which end of the knife to grab. Marty Symond. This is his style. Definitely. The viciousness. Preying on a poor defenseless animal.

And his skank drummer too, for that fucking matter, Dougy Bennett. He used to be big, used to be the drummer for Sobibor. The metal band? No? Man, you really *don't* listen to music. Well he was with Marty for a while, but he lost an eye. Tried to keep playing but his depth perception was gone. I mean he reaches for the high hat and he goes Whoa! I'm not hittin' anything! Where the fuck am I? And meanwhile he's lost the beat and the guys are all pissed off.

Well, that's a story. He was at Jerry's, the deli on Ventura, at four in the fucking morning, I don't gotta tell you what kind of fucking shape he's in, and he passes out. And I mean, plop, his head hits his sandwich and yeah, okay, who cares, except the little toothpick with the cellophane goes right into his fucking eye. They said they could have saved the eye if he'd gone to the hospital right away, but the waiters let him lie on the sandwich for half a fucking hour. I guess he was a regular.

I think so, yeah. Yeah, he still eats there.

Oh yeah, you like that picture? That's the NARAS Executive of the Year Dinner, Penta Hotel, two years ago. Guess who the Executive of the Year was? Goddamn right. Each of these people paid a thousand bucks to honor my ass. Thousand bucks a plate. Not bad for a boy from Cleveland, huh? These are really, these are my best friends in the business. I'm just looking at this thing . . . Really, it could've been anyone here. You should take it with you, the names are at the bottom.

Look at this guy, this is Vytautis Allosperios. *Legend*. Industry *legend*. Veets, I call him. Great old man. Has lunch at the same booth at the Polo Lounge every day. Very cultured. But also funky. Recorded Toscanini, but also recorded Rev. Gary Smalls. First guy to offer contracts to Diaspora, House Lights, The Lugnuts. Now this is a guy, all class. He wouldn't've done it. He might've *had* someone do it. No, I'm kidding. Not Veets. Although he did say to me once, we were arguing, he calls me "a disgrace, even to *this* industry," which I thought was uncalled for. Putting down your own industry. What's *that* about. But in fairness, it was during a dispute, tempers running, you know, heat of negotiation. Or renegotiation. Ordinarily a very dignified guy. Don't put his name down. You don't wanna spell it anyway.

But look at this guy, Larry Kirchenbauer, he works for me, hates my fucking guts—ha-ha-ha! That's okay. At this retreat once—we have these annual retreats for "strategic planning"—strategic bullshit is what it is, strategic fucking excuse to spend three days in the Caribbean—at the end of the retreat I give all my executives presents. Sometimes nice, sometimes a little gag gift, always heartfelt. Because it is a human business. It is a people business. Well, Larry, you gotta understand, he's this gay guy, obviously gay, but it's always "My girlfriend this" or "An old girlfriend that," always some line of bullshit. So last year, at our little farewell dinner, I give him one of those closet organizers, those things with all the compartments, I say, We all love you, Larry, and we want you to be comfortable in there. Everybody laughs except Larry, and he turns the color of, like in succession, he turns the colors of all the Jimis on the cover of *Smash Hits*. And then he runs—Jimi Hendrix. And then he runs out of the restaurant. Now, what *is* this shit? I mean I believe, officer, if you cannot laugh at yourself you are done in this business. *Finito*. Actually that's not true. There are a lot of people in this business who cannot laugh at themselves. Shit, who am I kidding. Some of them do very nicely. But if you cannot laugh at yourself, officer, here is the point, if you cannot laugh at yourself you are done as a *human being*. Without humor, what. What are we, officer? Without humor, we are animals. This is what this mungaloid Larry Kirchenbauer does not understand. I try to teach. This is a teaching company. And it is a fun company. And we do good things. A good product. And we learn, and we laugh.

Thank you, Constancia. When. That's good. Stop. When. *Gracias*.

Look at these guys. Look at these fucking guys. You know what the trouble is with the recording industry today? Look at the picture, it's right there, man. It's all in that picture. You see? You see—right there, man, and there and there and there. The socks. Exactly—*what* socks! Half of these fucking executives are not wearing socks. What is it with these fucks? I meet these young executives, you know, the blow-dried hair, the no socks, I just want to punch their faces in. Right the fuck in. I mean I want to grab them and scream, Look, man, who told you that here in Western civilization at this moment, at this juncture in time, modern man is gonna quit wearing stockings? What is this bullshit? You mean to tell me your fucking feet don't sweat? Jesus, all I can think about when I look at these fucks is what it's like when they take their shoes off at the end of the day. Jesus. I don't even want to shake their hands, I associate the hand sweat with the, uh, you know what I'm saying. Acch. I told one of 'em who works for us, I said, Look, you fuck, maybe you'd be happier at a socks-optional company. A company where they're interested in your fucking ankles. Because I, frankly, am not. And I put out a directive—some people thought it was a gag, but it was no fucking gag, officer, because it's not just the socks, it's not just the fucking socks, it's the smug fucking attitude that goes with the no socks, so I put out a directive, a fucking company-wide memo, that said that this company has a fucking dress code. And the dress code is socks. I don't give a shit if you walk in here wearing nothing *but* socks. But you will wear fucking socks. You will wear fucking socks if you work at this company. You will wear socks.

It is hipness, officer, that will kill this great industry. I am as hip as the next person. But I am from fucking *Cleveland*. I am grounded. And again I return to this whiz whiz whiz, this balloon shooting around the room. This is what the no socks is. These sockless people, they have no center. They would not fuck you in the ass when your back is turned. As any true business-person would. Because this is a goddamn business, officer. I will fuck you in the ass faster than you can say Patti fucking Page. Present your ass to me, officer, and this is what will happen. In a business context. Power intercourse. So don't give me this no fucking socks. This fucking piety. This fucking—

Now speaking of hip, look at this asshole, Johnny di Giaimo. Runs Sirocco Records. He should go on your fucking list, he should go quite high, perhaps a third of the way down or perhaps a little higher, one quarter or one eighth to one third of the way down. Now here's a guy, Mr. fucking Cocaine Party, Mr. fucking Disco, Mr. John di fucking Giaimo, here's a fucking guy, a good portion of the net of Sirocco Records from 1974 to 1980 he stored in his fucking nose. For safekeeping I'm sure he'll tell you, like how're the fucking creative accountants gonna dig it out of his fucking nostrils, although *his* accountants, I gotta tell you, if anyone can, you gotta hand it to him. Anyway, this is Mr. Open Shirt and Chains here, Mr. Dig My Sternum. His favorite pose is, go in his office and look at the pictures on his fucking walls, he's between two musicians, arms around both guys to spread his shirt open so you can see his hairy Italian chest. Now this is the fucking guy, this is the guy who was *behind* the Dennis Christian Turner thing, I fucking know it, he was the one who signed him the very fucking day after the courts dissolved my contract with him. Now *you* figure it out. And this is why I do not really blame DCT. And DCT is the only reason his fucking label survived the end of disco. And then later, credit where credit is due, they did get into hip-hop.

Not that they know shit about hip-hop. They bought Swang!, they didn't know shit themselves. So in the newer pictures there's Johnny between a couple of street kids, shirt still spread open, arms around shoulders but, you know, like Jimi on *Axis: Bold as Love*, that Indian thing, two more arms digging into these fucking kids' pockets. Otherwise he's the same. Except he's got knockers now. Still doesn't know shit about music. He doesn't know shit except how to steal money. Oh fuck, he doesn't even know *that*, his guy Myron Wax over there, Myron figures that shit out. And I take my hat off to him. I love Myron. I kid Myron, I say Hey Myron I hear you just signed II Turds Inna Wawa, I hear they're gonna be big. He laughs, I laugh. II Turds Inna Wawa. You know, with the Roman numeral II.

Which speaking of which, incidentally, that's exactly what I thought they were. When I first saw it. I mean, how the hell am I gonna know what they are? I come into the house, I don't know anything's wrong, I go to pee in there, go lift up the lid, and I think—Jesus! Somebody had a—what—a bloody stool? Is that what those are? Two little pieces of—you know, they're in the toilet, you have that association. Jesus. And then I see the what, the ganglia, what have you, whatever. Trailing off. Oy.

They cut 'em off and throw 'em in the toilet. Unbelievable. And then don't flush. What's *that* about. Unbelievable.

You know, and he's a pet. A purebred, sure, but I didn't get him for breeding. So what's the point. So hurtful. *So* hurtful.

And this is what it is. The hurt. This is the point. This in itself, the hurt, is the point. This was, in this sick fuck's mind, this was an eloquent, uh—Oh yes, thank you, Constancia. Yes, you can take it. *Finito*. Go ahead. Thank you . . . Lovely woman. Now *her* I like. A real person, there's a mensch, not like these—let me tell you, officer, that's *one* person you don't have to put on the list. I'll tell you that. Although who knows. Maybe way down the list. Who knows. Who knows what these people think.

A MORTY STORY

Uncle Morty asked to stay at my place last summer when he was coming to New York on a buying trip. He didn't want to pay fancy New York prices for a hotel. I said sure. I get along with Uncle Morty.

I asked my girlfriend, Astrid, if it was okay, not mentioning that I'd already said yes to Uncle Morty. It didn't matter because she said fine. She'd met him once and didn't mind him at all, and we have an extra little bedroom.

It was a hot day. The intercom buzzer sounded. I said, "Hello?"

"Hello, it's Uncle Morty. I'm here."

"Okay, Uncle Morty, I'll be right down." I'm on a third-floor walk-up and have to go down to let people in because there's no lock release on the intercom.

Uncle Morty had a little soft-sided suitcase and a worn brown briefcase. "Hello, it's Uncle Morty."

"Hiya, Morty, come on in." Uncle Morty is short and stocky

and dark, with thick glasses. We went upstairs and Morty shook Astrid's hand. Astrid is tall and blond.

Morty said, "Morty Ruskin."

"You've met Astrid, Uncle Morty."

"Sure. I didn't know if she remembered."

"Your room is in here."

Later I said, "What do you want for dinner, Uncle Morty?"

"Oh, anything. You keep kosher, don't you?"

Uncle Morty had breakfast cereal. We offered to go out and get him kosher meat, but he insisted that the cereal was fine. The three of us sat on stools behind the kitchen counter and watched *Matlock*. Morty said, through a mouthful of cereal, "If she'd killed her husband she never would've left the gun. It's a weakness."

Morty left for his business the next morning before we got up. The bathroom was still steamy when I went in. Astrid got some kosher chicken that day. Morty returned at about five, carrying his worn brown briefcase, his tie loosened. It was still pretty hot.

When we were alone for a moment Morty said to me with his big unblinking stare, "Your girlfriend—is her name *Trudy* or *Judy*?"

"It's Astrid, Uncle Morty."

"Oh. Okay."

We ate watching TV again. Uncle Morty ate everything Astrid put in front of him, eyes glued to the TV. Afterward he insisted that he would wash the dishes. He asked Astrid if she had an apron. Up with the pillowcases and stuff she found one that released closet smells when she unfolded it. Morty stood at the sink in the creased apron, his sleeves rolled up, washing the dishes. Sweat beaded his temples. I was glad he was doing it. It gets hot in there.

I think it was the next morning there was a knock at our bedroom door. I put on a bathrobe and came out. Uncle Morty was wearing only his glasses and a towel around his waist. "The stopper inside the bathtub won't come up." He followed me into the bathroom. "I'm trying to take a shower and the water won't drain out." It was because the little lever that opens the drain gets stuck sometimes. You just have to play with it. I showed Uncle Morty, who stood staring through his glasses, his hands clasped behind his back, his belly pushed out.

I got back into bed but couldn't fall asleep.

For some reason Uncle Morty had reminded me of Edward G. Robinson. His face didn't particularly look like Edward G.'s. His lips weren't quite as big. And of course he didn't talk in that snarly way. But he had that short square-bellied body and his nipples were big and saggy with dark hair sworled around them. Not that I knew what Edward G. Robinson's nipples looked like.

Astrid was awake so I told her about it. She said, "You sound disturbed by it."

"It doesn't bother you?"

"Why should it?"

"Well, him and his body there, with his glasses on, waiting for the shower?"

". . . Yeah?"

Other than that, things went along okay. One day Uncle Morty told us he wouldn't be home for dinner. A friend had told him about the kosher dairy restaurant on Seventy-second

Street and he was going to try it. Since Astrid, who was worried about the noise, didn't like having sex when Morty was in the house, we had it while he was gone. As I lay there afterward I imagined Uncle Morty in the kosher dairy restaurant, reading a folded-back newspaper through his big dark-framed glasses as he spooned borscht into his mouth.

The next day he ate at home again. I made spaghetti, which was a mistake because the kitchen alcove got all steamed up. We watched an old episode of *Cheers*. Uncle Morty's eyes were fixed on the TV as he lifted forkfuls of spaghetti to his mouth. He said, through a mouthful, "She was wearing a different dress the previous scene. It's the same day, though. What, she brings a change? It's a weakness."

In the evening Uncle Morty sat in the living room and read the paper and then a book about the history of China. I read a book called *Captured by the Indians*, a collection of first-hand accounts. Astrid was reading a murder mystery.

Morty fell asleep. His mouth gaped and his head lolled back, the overhead light sheeting his glasses. His hair, thinning at the crown, was tufted as if someone had gathered it into a fist and given it a long hard clench. He started snoring. At first the snores were just the dry rattle of breath sawing across his throat. Then, as he sucked more energetically, the snores warmed and moistened into a loud snarfing sound. They subsided for a mysterious moment, leaving the muted whoosh of distant traffic. Then they slammed back in, loud flaps of flesh and phlegm.

I was giggling. Astrid sat with her eyes fixed grimly on her book. I must say this pissed me off. She even silently shook her head, a judgment upon me.

Suddenly Morty strangled on a snore, his throat seizing up on an overly greedy inhale. He gagged, elaborately. His eyes shot open, and after a stupefied moment, his head swung round the room.

By the time I felt his eyes reach me I was looking back down at my book. I was still silently laughing, but my eyeline and an appreciative waggle of my head indicated some whimsy in the book. After a moment Morty cleared his throat and said:

"Dozed off."

I looked up, with Astrid.

"Did you?" she said.

Uncle Morty would telephone home. As Astrid and I sat reading and traffic noise floated in he would say "Honey? Honey? It's me. Honey?" He talked loud, as if they had just invented the telephone. "How is everything? Honey? How're the kids? How's Yaffee?" Yaffee was their dog. "Honey?"

"Say, you know," Morty said one day, "you don't have any fruit in the refrigerator." We have never had fruit in the refrigerator. We don't have stuff in the refrigerator. We go out and get stuff for dinner, night by night. Morty wasn't complaining, though. He wouldn't complain. He was only warning us that there was no fruit in the refrigerator.

. . .

I was laughing one day, just laughing, like a person will. Astrid said, "What?"

"I was just—I don't know. I was just thinking."

"What?"

"I was picturing Uncle Morty climbing up the stairs here to the apartment, with his briefcase, but he didn't have any arms and legs. Like that guy in *Freaks*. He was just wriggling up the stairs, you know, holding the briefcase handle in his teeth. Just a torso, you know. Wearing a diaper. Wriggling up the stairs."

"That's funny?"

"Well you know, he was still Uncle Morty, perfectly happy, coming home from work. He just didn't have any arms and legs. 'Honey? Honey? It's a weakness!' You know, still the same."

Astrid looked at me. She shook her head at me, which was bullshit, as if she were defending him, as if she were on his side and I wasn't. I like Uncle Morty. It wasn't a hostile thing.

It was the day for Morty to leave. He kissed Astrid goodbye, a little peck. I walked him down the stairs carrying his suitcase. At the door we shook hands and he told me to take care. He also said, "That girl Astrid is wonderful." This really pissed me off.

Later in the day we discovered that Morty had left us towels as a gift. A couple of months later Astrid dumped me.

A FEVER IN THE BLOOD

He was trying to bite my ear off.

His jaw was clamped over it and his breath was hot and moist. He was grunting and snarling like a junkyard dog with last night's T-bone.

"Right," I said, "no girls' rules."

I jerked a knee up into his groin. Hard. He doubled over but kept his jawhold. My head went down with his. I landed a right that even at close quarters had enough on it to snap his jaw shut and send it rocketing back. That was a tactical mistake. My ear came off clean with the punch.

The hell with it.

He was staggering back, hands stretched behind him, groping for support. I put everything into a kick at his kneecap. He danced and crumpled like a marionette whose puppeteer has a stroke. Some of the fight was out of him now. But he would be back up and at me if I gave him half a chance.

With one fluid motion I crossed my arms over my chest and

sent my hands under my coat. The left came out holding a hankie. I pressed it against the side of my head. The right came out holding a Webley .45. You can bet it kicked and roared.

He spat my ear ten feet high.

"Take it to hell with my curse," I bellowed. "And tell all the other poor damned souls that Victor Strang means business!"

But it was as if someone had stopped up my mouth with a towel. My voice thundered inside my head, but the only sound in the alleyway was the echo of the gun blast. And it roared and roared.

And it roared.

I woke up sweating. White. Everywhere white. A woman in white smiled down.

Hospital.

The room was quiet—dead quiet; all ambient sound had been sucked away. I reached up to touch my right ear and felt only a thick bandage taped to the side of my head. At my touch it shot back bolts of pain.

The bastard. Bit it off clean. I'd drilled him, passed out, and gone to . . . the dream. A train station. Clanking. Echoes. And now . . .

I wiped the sweat from my eyes.

The nurse was moving her lips at me, but the dead room swallowed up all her noise. It didn't seem to bother her. Why should it bother me? I looked up at the ceiling. Tiles with rows and rows of little holes. How many holes in the whole ceiling. The hole ceiling. The whole ceiling.

No noise came out when I screamed.

I screamed again, but the room sucked my voice away.

Something wet and furry hit my arm.

Only the nurse, swabbing my arm with cotton. I hadn't heard her reach for me. Behind her a doctor squinted up at a syringe. They were going to send me back under.

The nurse looked frightened. Why? I would never hurt her. I would never let anyone hurt her. Her soft face floated under long blond curls. As she sat and held my forearm I could see up her dress. She had firm and gentle thighs. A man could build a life there. I looked at them and cried. I cried without noise.

They were going to send me back to the dream. But I wanted to stay here, with her. I wanted her to unbutton her uniform and press me to her bosom, heal me, whisper in my ear. I wanted to feel her warm breath whistling in my ear.

"Marry me!" I bellowed at her. "Marry me! Marry me!"

The doctor jabbed me.

The nurse didn't unbutton her uniform. She didn't press me to her bosom. And I didn't have an ear for her to whisper in.

My head dropped away.

Thoughts struggled to the surface, fighting for air. When they took off the bandage what would my earhole look like? Would my brains show? Would they get dry and crusty, like the toothpaste when you leave off the cap? My eyelids were ten-ton weights.

They went down and I went with them.

Clank . . . Like steam through a radiator, far away. Darkness. Dripping narrow stone walls. *Clank* . . .

"Quickly!" It is the three little men. The men in red. Redcaps. They stand right in front of me, but their voices come from far, far away. "Quickly!"

They skitter ahead and wave in unison for me to follow. They carry conductor's lanterns. They wear red flowing robes. "The pontiff is a busy man!" Not redcaps—cardinals! Now I remember. "Quickly!" Not a train station—a church!

"I am not a Catholic." My own dull voice booms against my ears. The cardinals scurry on and I follow, taking drugged, leaden steps. But not losing ground. Slower than them, but not losing ground.

In unison they wave again, their lanterns swaying. From up the corridor comes a low, pitiful wail. Then a wave of roaring laughter. It echoes off the stone and dies into the wind. We are emerging into the basilica. "I am not a Catholic. I am not—"

We are there.

He is bathed in dust-filtered light. He lies on his back on a red vinyl bench. He grunts as his elbows jerk straight over his head, and weights clank against the bar.

Three other cardinals are leading another man away. The man is pressing a towel to his face. From behind he looks just like me.

Poor bastard, whoever he is.

"Phhhhh." *Clank*. The pope drops the barbell onto the Y rest over his head. It echoes. He sits up on the red vinyl bench, smiles at me. "*Viene, viene.*" His voice echoes, bounces off every wall.

I climb the stairs.

His gym shorts extend to just above his knobbed knees. He wears a ribbed sleeveless undershirt. He towels the perspiration from his underarms, then his forehead. At a corner of the towel is an embroidered red *P*. The pope smiles.

"Kneel."

Turn. Run.

I kneel.

He reaches out and strokes my hair. I look behind me. The three cardinals stand with their hands clasped in front of them, heads cast respectfully down. Hypocrites! As if they didn't know!

"My son . . ."

Only there are more of them now, more than three. The basilica is filled with them, a sea of heads cast respectfully down. Cardinals. Hypocrites! Monsignors. Hypocrites! Bishops, primates, prelates, monks—an army of hypocrites, a wild harvest, a solemn riot of fantastic hats.

"I am a Lutheran"—my voice cracks—"born in Fargo-Moorhead."

"My son . . ." He is extending the back of his hand toward my face. "You may kiss our ring." An enormous signet ring. I have seen this before. I have seen this ring. I will see it a hundred times more before my life is through.

I recoil—not in time.

As the jet of water shoots from the ring and catches me in the eye, the pope chuckles.

The clergymen throw their heads back.

And roar.

My face was warm. I moved my head, dozed. Still warm. I opened my eyes.

Sunlight was streaming in the window. The white room was still quiet, quiet on top of quiet.

I said it, not knowing whether I said it aloud. "I am deaf."

The doctor, sitting beside my bed, holding a notepad in his lap, nodded.

I felt my voice rumble through my throat: "Why? Why? The bastard in the alley only got one ear."

The doctor wrote on his notepad and handed it to me. "Nothing organically wrong with your left ear. Psychological deafness. Hysterical reaction. Not uncommon after severe bodily trauma."

At least he could hear me.

I looked around the room. A white-haired old guy was in the next bed, staring at me. His hands were shaking. One good sneeze would kill him.

The doctor touched my arm and showed me the pad: "That's Mr. Levant. He used to be a very important business-man." The doctor smiled.

"Where's that nurse?"

The doctor looked at me funny. Then he wrote: "She asked to be transferred to another ward."

Huh.

I said: "Will I have to learn Braille?"

He shook his head. Of course not.

I'm not such a big reader anyway.

Two policemen were in the room. They showed me their badges. They wrote questions about the bastard. They asked me if I'd been working on a case, so they must have gone through my things and found my PI's license. I told them no, that I'd never seen the guy before. They wrote that his name was Johnny Marchetta, that he'd been one of Ray Scalese's punks, all of which was news to me. I couldn't tell them anything and they didn't much care; my ear made it justifiable homicide open and shut. They asked me if I had any idea why he'd bitten it off. I told them no, which was the truth at the time. I didn't know then that it was something in the Marchetta blood.

The doctor couldn't tell me how long I'd be deaf. The right ear was a total loss, but the left ear was mental, and about the mind you never can tell. When he discharged me the doctor suggested I take the sign language course at the Y. Finger waving. Fat chance. Bad enough I couldn't even hear myself talk. All the deaf people I ever heard, they sound like Gomer Pyle on downers. The doctor gave me the name of a psychiatrist he said might be able to help me hear. Yeah. Probably his brother-in-law. I was just happy to leave Croak Central.

I watched a lot of television. The high point of the day was the captioned news. I'd go for long walks in the park. When I saw people staring at me I knew I'd been singing. One day I got hit in the head with a Frisbee. I turned around and saw a kid running toward me, holding his arms up, saying something. I beat the hell out of him.

At the end of the week I still couldn't hear so I went to the psychiatrist.

He actually had me lie down on a couch and close my eyes

while I talked, which struck me as corny but who was I to judge. He wrote for me to tell about my childhood and my dreams, as these were supposed to be important. I did, three times a week, fifty minutes. He'd sit behind me and listen. Sometimes I really didn't have anything to say and I'd just lie on the couch until he walked in front of me and smiled and pointed at his watch—time to go.

I began wondering whether all of this was doing me any good. I didn't start hearing again, that's for damn sure. One session I asked the psychiatrist wasn't he supposed to do something besides sit there and draw pay, but he wrote back why was I hostile. I asked how come I couldn't just lie on the couch at home and tell my childhood to the walls, and he shook his jowls and clutched his gut like it was the best one he'd heard all week.

Well, I couldn't afford to be a deadbeat until my hearing came back and I was sick of sitting around feeling sorry for myself. I started going in to my office every morning. I sat there behind my desk and watched the door. I didn't want to be staring off into space like an idiot when a client walked in.

I stared at that door for three days before it opened.

She looked maybe thirty, but it's hard to tell with fat people. She hovered at the doorway like she was afraid to come in. I nodded at the chair in front of my desk. She gave a little smile, said something, shut the door behind her, and sat down. Her face looked strained.

She started right in. It looked like she was talking pretty fast. She kept her eyes fixed on the front of my desk as she talked. She kneaded the purse in her lap, her hands getting more and more worked up. Once in a while she would shoot a glance up at me without a break in her talking. A tear dropped into her lap. Then another. Her chin shook. Then both chins. She was bawling away pretty good now but still talking on through it. She fumbled at the clasp on her purse and took out a photo and pushed it across the desk. It was a heavyset cheerful-looking guy about her age. I guess it was her husband. I looked back at her. She was still talking, but settling down a bit. She was dabbing at her eyes with a handkerchief. Finally she blew her nose into the handkerchief, opened it, studied it, recrumpled it, stuffed it back in her purse, and stopped talking. We both just sat for a moment. She was looking at me. Expectantly.

"Lady," I said. "I don't hear a word you're saying."

Her face froze. She stared at me.

I'd have to tell her everything now.

"I had a little accident a couple of weeks ago." I pointed to the bandage on the side of my head. "Got my ear bit off by a bastard named Marchetta. I'm deaf, but I'm a perfectly good private investigator, and if you'll just write down whatever it is you want done"—I pushed my notepad and pen across the desk—"I'll get right on it." She didn't make any move to pick up the pad. She had the same look, expectant, only now her face looked harder, chiseled, like she was done moving it around for the day. "My fee is a hundred a day and expenses, with an itemized bill and receipts." She sat there, staring at me. You'd think my nose was bit off too. "If I don't produce a receipt, you don't pay for that expense." She looked at the notepad. She looked at me. She looked at the notepad. She looked at me. "Overhead is my headache. If you—"

She jumped out of her chair, reached across the desk, grabbed the photo out of my hand, and trundled out the door, slamming it behind her. Hell.

I'd handled that one all wrong.

I gazed out the window at the building across the street. How much longer would I have to wait before another client came through the door? In an office across the street a secretary was putting on nail polish. I wondered: Could she love a man with one ear? That might sound like a silly question to you, but I was thinking that maybe she could. Not right away, of course, but maybe she could learn to love him.

The curtains were sucked out the window. A draft. I looked over to the opened door. The fat woman was standing in it, moving her lips. From the cords in her neck and the way she was hunched forward I could tell she was shouting. Then she left again, shutting the door hard enough to make the floor shake. "Same to you, lady," I hollered. Some people have no feeling for the handicapped. I'd expected better from someone who was no prize herself.

That afternoon turned out to be my last visit to the psychiatrist. I was lying on the couch talking about the time I almost drowned in the Muscatatuck River when I was eight years old. I didn't know how much the story would mean to him, not knowing whether he was familiar with the Fargo area. I craned around to ask him.

He was slouched in his swivel chair with his feet propped up on the desk, laughing and talking into the telephone.

"Hey."

When he saw me he straightened up real quick and cradled the telephone. He clasped his hands together on the desk. He looked down at his hands, then back up at me. He smiled.

How much of that session had he spent on the phone? How much of all my sessions? Half? More than half? All?

I got to my feet, slow, and walked over to his desk. I must have looked mad. God knows I felt it. The psychiatrist's smile left his face and he nervously poked around the desktop. He picked up my file and started examining it. He shot a glance up at me. I guess he was trying to figure out what to do. He acted real busy reading the file. He pursed his lips, looking at it, then shot me a stupid grin.

When I reached out he flinched like he thought I was going to belt him one, but I didn't. I yanked the file out of his hand. Inside there was a sheet of paper with "Strang, Victor" typed at the top. Underneath he had handwritten "Deaf." In the middle of the sheet was a little drawing of a log cabin with a stick man standing in front of it, and under that was a scribbled note. "Drinks. Miriam. 8:45."

That was it. My whole goddamn file.

Maybe you think I didn't blow.

I called him names. When I ran out of names I started screaming. When I got too hoarse to scream I tipped over his desk which was not easy, believe me. But the funny thing was how he just sat there, staring at his pipe, wincing but never looking at me, like if only he didn't look at me maybe I wouldn't sock him. If that was the idea, it worked. I never did belt the guy. I just kicked the desk a couple times and stormed out. His receptionist had been standing in the doorway gawking at me. She got out of my way fast.

That was the worst day of my life up till then. I called the Better Business Bureau to tell them the whole story of the ride I'd been taken for. I don't know if they ever did anything about the guy. I don't even know if they answered the phone.

God, but time went slow.

I didn't want a repeat of the scene with the fat woman, so I called a sign painter and had him stencil HEARING-IMPAIRED on the pebbled-glass door between VICTOR STRANG and PRIVATE INVESTIGATOR. I bought one of those phone-answering machines and recorded a message: "This is Victor Strang. My secretary is out at the moment and I am temporarily deaf. You may contact me in person at my office or you may leave a message after the tone, which my secretary will transcribe when she returns." I gave the cleaning woman twenty bucks to check the machine every night.

What with the money I was giving her, and the four hundred eighty I'd dropped on the psychiatrist, and the forty bucks for the sign painter, and the seventy-five for the answering machine, not to mention the six hundred for the hospital, the ear business was running some dough. I thought of suing the estate of Johnny Marchetta, but I doubted he had an estate. Even if he did my lawyer would probably screw me. Why not, I was deaf.

Truth in advertising sure as hell didn't help business. After two more weeks of waiting I figured I'd be grateful for anything. So what finally comes in? A guide hitch, with a German shepherd at one end and a joker in shades at the other.

Terrific.

I escorted him to the chair in front of my desk and asked if he realized that I was hearing-impaired. He nodded. I asked how he proposed we communicate. His fingers made little pecking motions at the desk.

"You type?"

He nodded. I pulled my old Underwood out from the top shelf of the coat closet, put it on the desk in front of the guy, fed in some paper, and put his hands on the keyboard for him.

He wrote, "U tgubj nt wufe us cgeatubg ub ne," and looked up at the spot on the wall to my left and smiled.

There are probably thousands of people in this town who are in trouble and need help from someone like me, and after three weeks of waiting I get Mr. Magoo.

"Mister," I said, "you speak English?" He frowned and nodded. "You write it?" He frowned and nodded again, and pointed at what he'd just typed.

"Mister," I said. I hope I was sounding more patient than I felt. "You just wrote, 'U tgubj nt wufe us cgeatubg ub ne.' That's no English I ever heard." He shook his head and started typing again. "Hold on, lamebrain, there's no paper in the carriage." That can really screw up the roller. I fed in another sheet. He was retyping. "U tgubj nt wufe . . . " when I noticed that the fingers of his right hand were resting on the wrong keys. I moved his hand over for him and asked him to start again. This time it came out "I think my wife is cheating on me." I read it out loud and he nodded. He typed, "Her name is Natalie." When I read that back the German shepherd jumped to its feet and started barking. The blind guy banged it across the snout and it lay down again.

"Okay, what's your name and address?"

He typed, "Kendall Dealy. 1618 Taliafero."

"Mr. Dealy . . . do you know what your wife looks like?"

He shook his head.

This was going to be tough.

"Do you have a picture of her?"

He nodded and took a picture out of his wallet and put it on the desk. It was a very grainy snapshot. Three men in round parkas were looking into the camera. Hoods and scarves obscured their faces. It was an Arctic scene. There was an American flag planted in the snow just behind them.

"Mr. Dealy," I said. "This is a picture of a goddamn polar expedition."

He hunched forward and groped toward my face. I put the picture in his hand. He held it out in front of his dog. The dog gave it a halfhearted sniff and began scratching itself. The blind guy typed, "I asked for a picture of her to keep in my wallet. She's a practical joker. I'll get a picture of her and mail it to you."

"That may not be necessary. I assume she's the only woman living in the house?" He nodded. "Then I'll just set up in front of your place and tail her whenever she leaves. I can start tomorrow." He nodded again. "A couple hundred would serve as a retainer." He fished out his wallet again and pulled out a wad of bills. He rubbed the upper right-hand corner of each bill before laying it on my desk. I looked at the bills. They had little pinpricks in the corner indicating, I supposed, the denomination. Clever.

I said, "All right, Mr. Dealy—" but he started typing again.

"Call me Ken. The dog's name is Turk."

"Fine," I said. "Fine."

It was a start. It was something. It was a paying client. Maybe I could build up a livable trade off the wingdings and goofballs and dumbskies until my hearing came back. What the hell, maybe develop a specialized little rep.

So I was feeling half all right when I took the elevator up from lunch, and even more so when I thought I saw another customer. An old guy in a raincoat was standing in the hall outside my office. I eyeballed him as I walked up. He seemed to fit the new consumer profile: vacant eyes, mouth hanging open, hands worming around in his coat pockets. He was moving his lips at me. I pointed at the sign on my door and said, "Sorry, I—" and then he drew the gun.

He said, "All right, then I'll give it to you right here in the hall."

I know that's what he said because I heard him say it.

I took one look at that gun and heard everything—all of a sudden, like when the refrigerator goes on in the middle of the night. I heard traffic from the street. I heard people typing down the hall. I heard the rustle of the old man's coat. To me it was music. To me it was Mozart.

"Who are you?" My own voice didn't stop at my throat now.

It flooded the inside of my head, splashed against my ears, and washed down the hallway.

He said, "I'm Pops Marchetta. I just got back from Honolulu." He licked his lips. "Ray Scalese told me what you done." He raised the gun.

I didn't think—I just decked him with a right. His gun skated down the hall. I heard it clatter away. I heard the old man hit the floor. It felt good, hearing. It felt fine. It felt so good I bent down to help the old bastard up.

He whipped both arms around my neck and yanked my head down to his. He said, "My Johnny was a good boy." For an old man he was plenty strong.

His jaw clamped over my left ear. I heard gurgles in his throat.

THE BOYS

Why the Crazy Horse Pageant? But Davey had even managed to get Bart—phlegmatic Bart—worked up about it. The poster said that it would be mounted on the fairgrounds outside of Vermillion, South Dakota on August 17, in three days' time, just at the end of their camping trip. The poster had been up for so long that it was already difficult to make out the list of events that constituted the daylong show, but apparently it was a celebration in drama, recitation, and Native American song of the life and times of the great Lakota war chief. It was to start at nine in the morning.

The father tasted bile in the back of his throat as soon as Davey started talking about it. Clearly the word "pageant" had tripped something in Davey's brain and he was mad to go. When told that they couldn't, he kept saying, "Dad, I would understand if there was a *reason*." The father was infuriated both by the insufferable expression and because although there *was* a reason, it was one of pure punishing inconvenience, and that was a concept no eight-year-old could be brought to understand. Going to the pageant would mean getting up at six o'clock to strike the tent and pack the camping gear, and driving an hour and a half in the opposite direction from home. If they in fact stayed all day the three of them would have to spend an extra night sleeping together in a crummy motel on the way back.

He remembered the chlorine-scented motel room on the way to the campsite, in which he'd sat rigidly in a chair damped by one of the children's swimsuits trying to read a book but managing only to stare at one page while listening to the clunk and hum of a distant ice machine. He was thinking then about the variety of irritating tasks that he knew the camping trip held in store: He would have to blow up air mattresses, clear stones from beneath one child's air mattress, pretend to clear stones from beneath the aggrieved other child's air mattress, build a fire, make the fire bigger, make the fire smaller, make the fire a different shape, accompany each child to the latrine in the middle of the night, hyperextend his shoulder groping important toys and fetishes from beneath the car seat, swab soda pop and sick-up off the upholstery, and otherwise cater to the children's needs real and imagined while listening to Davey's nonstop suggestions and complaints. He had managed to work himself into a vibrating rage of self-recrimination for consenting to take the boys to the Black Hills when a man in the room next door had had a trumpeting bowel movement. Davey had screamed with laughter. Bart remained sitting on the vinyl sofa at the front of the room, engrossed in his Sesame Street catalog. Later the three of them had gone to dinner in a café attached to the motel, Bart eating rice, Davey slurping down a mucilaginous beef Stroganoff, and the father picking at a club sandwich; and later still with the children asleep next to him, their arms outflung and mouths agape, the father had sat in bed watching a fuzzed-over TV talk show with the volume turned low. The guests, the usual whores and crybabies in the movie business, did not interest him, but the inane show did somehow turn his leaping fury into smaller waves of anger and depression that rippled over his body like water over a smooth flat stone.

The little boy, Bart, who had finally learned how to talk but chose to do so only at odd moments, was three years younger than Davey and had developed an obsessive interest in Sesame Street. He enjoyed all of the books and videos, but for some months now his chiefest interest had been in a catalog of the Sesame Street products. He preferred the catalog to any of the products themselves and would sit hunched over it for an hour at a time, carefully examining each page. When he reached the last page he would gaze at it, turn it, study the back cover at length, then flip the catalog over and start again. He insisted that his parents mend with Scotch tape each small tear, and by virtue of this and the many dog-ears and wrinkles that had accumulated over the months, the catalog was now about twice its original thickness.

When Bart had learned that there was a Sesame Street theme park called Sesame Place, in Pennsylvania, he had agitated to visit it and, when told that it was too far to visit, had had a disturbing tantrum. His body had gone rigid and the cords in his neck stood out, and first his face and then his entire body turned red. Temper tantrums like this, worse than any he had ever had before, became chronic. They came to so overwhelm his body that his parents worried that they were seizures of some sort. They took Bart to the pediatrician and triggered one by prying the Sesame Street catalog out of his hands. The doctor observed the fit and told them that it was not dangerous but suggested that perhaps the child was immature. Everyone except Bart had felt foolish.

But the lobbying to visit Sesame Place had not consisted only of tantrums. When Bart did talk it was of nothing else. Family life became a hellishly endless argument about Sesame Place; Bart was a rock, small, stolid, immovable, diverting the stream of every conversation toward the one Nirvana-like end. Finally the parents gave in and took a weekend holiday there, both of them bored, Davey indifferent, Bart in a trance. He wandered around clutching his catalog, eyes wide, soaking it in. His head made jerky robotic swings here and there to focus on each Sesame Street character that swam into view, depicted on signs, rides, gift displays, other visitors' T-shirts. Although Bart never smiled or in any other way appeared to be enjoying himself, he did leave the park with an air of deep soul satisfaction.

The camping trip went about as expected. The second to last night Davey did indeed wake his father to help him find his robe and escort him to the latrine; for some reason he would not urinate out-of-doors against a tree. Even in the latrine Davey would only pee once the father had found a stick to shoo away the sluggish and elaborately armored bugs that feast on dung, and then the father had to hold his flashlight trained on Davey's penis so he could see what he was doing. When they got back to the tent and the father had crawled back into his sleeping bag he was immediately called upon to rise again and return to the latrine path with the flashlight to find a card showing the Indian tribes of the Dakotas that had been in the pocket of Davey's robe, and as soon as he got back again, Bart decided that he too had to go to the latrine. Halfway there the father, fearing that he would have to spend another ten minutes patting the shells of dung bugs with a stick, convinced Bart to pee against a tree, but Bart ended up peeing largely into a flap of his robe, which then dripped down onto his shoe. The father had to rise early the next morning, in itself not a problem since he had never managed to fall back asleep, in order to rinse the robe and the shoe in the river before preparing breakfast. Breakfast involved the use of multiple pots and pans because Davey would have only oatmeal and Bart would throw a tantrum unless he had a jelly omelet. As he waited for the eggs to cook the father tried to puzzle out which of his life's missteps had brought him to this point, where he could only venture into the wild armed with an omelet pan and a large jar of Smucker's peach jelly. He tended to see himself, in these bitter and paranoid moments, as a rat in an elaborate and cruelly pointless behavioral experiment. Marriage, child rearing, even the physical act of sex appeared as quivering compulsions subject to the cool scrutiny of some higher clinician. His smoldering alienation, and the trip itself, reached a climax the next morning when, after the father had struck the tent, packed the car, and gotten about halfway to Vermillion, South Dakota, the fairgrounds of which were home to the Crazy Horse Pageant, Davey said, "Dad, car's burning."

It was true. Whenever they came to a stop smoke would plume from the undercarriage; resumed motion would whip the smoke away so that it was no longer visible. The father's jaw became rigid and his grip tightened on the wheel. He reduced his speed for the rest of the trip to Vermillion and eased the car into what seemed to be the town's only service station. A lined and grizzled man with the name EGON stitched onto engineer's overalls stared at the father through pale blue eyes while the father described the problem and Davey, standing next to him, gazed up. The mechanic curtly told the father that he would "diagnose it" and the father pulled Bart out of the backseat, where he was studying his Sesame Street catalog. Egon got into the car and, with his door still open and his left leg trailing outside, pulled it onto the hydraulic lift, leaving the father and Bart to sit in the service station office on metal chairs whose torn mint green upholstery sprouted dirty white stuffing. As Bart resumed his study of the Sesame Street catalog, the father picked up a copy of the Rapid City newspaper. He noted with irritation that it contained no news, only stories headlined INVESTORS STAND BY LANDFILL DEVELOPER, COUPLE'S GENEROSITY WILL SEND CHILD TO SUMMER CAMP, and the like, and that its two-page ARTS section consisted of a half page of small ads for hair-loss remedies and abridged wire service profiles of the usual whores and crybabies in the movie business. While he leafed through the paper a loud bell periodically clanged in the office as, outside, Davey hopped up and down on the tire belt.

Egon shortly came in wiping his hands on a rag, his crinkling gray hair spotted with black oil. Davey ran in after him and stood next to his father, laid one hand on his armrest, and stared up as Egon tersely explained the problem. The transmission, it seemed, was leaking fluid onto the exhaust pipe and the fluid burned off as the pipe heated up. It was a slow leak and Egon had put in a quart of transmission fluid; they could continue to use the car until it was convenient to get the leak fixed so long as they kept an eye on the fluid level. The father thanked him, paid him, and got, he thought, a particularly sour look when he asked for directions to the fairgrounds.

"Dad," said Davey when they were back in the car and driving again, "that guy had gunk in his hair."

It was after nine-thirty when they pulled into the large rutted field that was the fairgrounds parking lot. It was empty. A low stake fence separated the lot from the fairgrounds proper, which was another large rutted field, equally empty.

As Bart sat reading and the idling car plumed smoke, the father and Davey stared out at the bare field. Songbirds twittered.

"Dad, what's goin' on?"

On the drive back into town the scenery seemed to pulse as blood pounded behind the father's eyeballs. He pulled into the service station, where Egon emerged from the office, wiping his hands on an oily rag, his expression blank.

The father rolled down his window and stuck his head out and sucked in the hot air that wafted back across the hood, all its oxygen burned away. "Isn't there an Indian pageant out at the fairgrounds?"

Egon stared at him. "Last year."

. . .

Morning sun glared on the Formica and kicked off the chrome of the Vermillion Diner, where they decided to have breakfast before starting back. The father squinted up as the waitress arrived, and asked if she had any aspirin.

"We're not allowed to give customers aspirin."

". . . Why?"

"We could be sued."

The father nodded, as if acknowledging the statement's sense. At length he said, "I'll have the fruit salad." He nodded at Davey: "Oatmeal for him." He nodded at Bart: "And he'll have a two-egg omelet."

"He wants two eggs?"

"Yes."

"How does he want them?"

"Huh? An omelet."

". . . In almlet?"

"A*n* omelet, two-egg omelet."

"Um . . ."

"You know, an omelet."

". . . What's that?"

". . . You don't know what an omelet is?"

"No."

"Well, just tell the cook. He'll know. It's the eggs, like scrambled eggs, but you don't squish them around in the pan. An omelet."

"I'll ask . . ." Her voice was tight, as if she suspected a put-on.

When she left, Davey said, "Can't they make Bart an omelet, Dad?"

"They'll make an omelet." At home Bart's mother would slather the Smucker's peach jelly onto the nearly cooked eggs before folding them over, but they found that at restaurants which as a rule would not prepare jelly omelets, Bart would allow them to order a plain omelet, which they would then spread jelly on top of. But here, for the first time, was a place that did not serve omelets at all. And worse still, like a preposterously banal episode of *The Twilight Zone*, they had not even heard of them.

Bart liked rice as well. In fact, jelly omelets aside, he liked only rice. He would pour ketchup onto his rice and mash it in with a fork. They called it Spanish rice and once when they went out to a Spanish restaurant they had ordered Bart the real thing. He took one forkful, spat it out, and started screaming. The father slapped him, and Bart shrieked louder and flung his plate to the ground. The father yanked him up and hustled him out of the restaurant, stomping Spanish rice into the deep red carpet, Bart tucked under one arm like a football.

The waitress came back. "Well, the cook knows what it is, but we don't have it on the menu."

"Okay, but he can make one?"

"It's not on the menu."

"But the cook knows how to make them."

"I'm sorry, sir, it's not on the menu."

"Wait a minute. You went back there to see if he could make an omelet. He told you he *could* make an omelet. In fact, if anything, it's *less* work than scrambled eggs."

"I don't know about that." She matched the slowness of his

speech. "He does say he knows what they are. But. It's not on the menu, sir. We don't serve the almlet."

Davey was sniggering; Bart was still absorbed by his catalog.

"You knew it wasn't on the menu before. And yet you entertained the idea of serving one. You went to find out if you could. So, you were then entertaining the idea of serving something not on the menu."

The waitress squinted incomprehension. ". . . I *what?*"

The father choked down his rage. "All right," he said. "All right." He tried to concentrate. What would Adolf Hitler do in this situation? Or Joe Stalin? He tried to picture Hitler in the diner in a feed cap and overalls, stirring coffee at the counter, buttocks squashed against a stool. But it was hard to imagine what exactly Hitler would do. There were so many cultural differences.

"All right," said the father. "He'll have two scrambled eggs. And just ask the cook not to squish them around in the pan."

The waitress looked at him narrowly and, after a wordless moment, snapped the menu out of his hand and left.

"Are they gonna make Bart an omelet, Dad?"

"Yes."

The waitress was talking with the cook behind the counter as she clipped the order ticket onto a revolving metal wheel. The cook must have been a very short person; all that was visible was the top of a nodding white hat.

"She said they wasn't."

"She said they *weren't*. But they will."

"What's wrong? Are they dumbbells?"

The father sipped his coffee. The pain behind his eyes had dulled and the wave of irritation was receding, deep inside. He waited patiently for it to disappear, concentrating on it as it ebbed away, no longer threatened by it. He was in control now. It was faint, very faint; he was like a great yogi listening to his own heartbeat.

Presently the waitress returned. She put a bowl of oatmeal in front of Davey, a fountain glass filled with canned fruit in front of the father, and two eggs, fried, sunny side up, in front of Bart. She left.

Bart looked up from his Sesame Street catalog and stared at the glistening eggs. They vibrated slightly as a truck rumbled by outside.

The father watched with a cold clutch of fear, bracing himself for Bart's tantrum. He tried to still his dread by picturing himself muscling the waitress back through the swinging doors into the kitchen and, with one hand bending her arm back behind her, forcing her face down into a panful of frying eggs. He imagined giving her neck a vigorous whisking motion so that her nose whipped the eggs while she loudly blubbered.

But then, that would not be an omelet either.

As Bart continued to stare at the eggs the waitress returned with a small plate holding two pieces of limp white buttered toast, cut diagonally in half. "Comes with the eggs," she said, and walked away.

Bart, oddly, had not lost his equanimity. His eyes wandered over the table seeking, as it turned out, jelly; he reached a packet of it from the plastic caddy on which several were stacked. He picked up a piece of toast and carefully spread the jelly on it as it drooped around his hand; he rotated the hand in order to cover the entire piece. This done, he turned the piece over to spread jelly on its other side.

Davey was eating his oatmeal, his eyes on his brother's plate. "That's not an omelet," he said. "Are we gonna complain, Dad?"

Bart started eating the toast and went back to his catalog.

The father sipped his coffee.

"Dad? That's not an omelet."

Having eaten all the toast, Bart had started drinking the syrup out of his father's fruit salad. He had choked on it rather theatrically and gotten a great deal of both the syrup and his own drool on his T-shirt, so the father had helped him to take it off, Bart holding his catalog first in one hand and then the other as each arm was pulled free.

Bart ambled on ahead to the car as the father and Davey went to the register to pay. The waitress rang up the bill and, while accepting their money, gave them a rote "Was everything satisfactory?"

The father stared at her.

Davey looked at his father, looked at the waitress, grasped that the bridge of communication had been blown, and tossed his own rope across the chasm: "Nuh-uh, lady—that wasn't an omelet."

The father grimaced as contempt gave way to pity in the woman's face. Clearly she was thinking that Davey was a brat, but that little more could be expected from a child with such a boorish parent. The father felt his muscles knot. He wanted to strike both her and the child.

This, though, was Davey. A more mysterious part of the boy was his screaming nightmares; he was never able to say what they were about. They suggested that some of his odder behavior was terror-averting. He had once meticulously copied the periodic table out of an encyclopedia, all the elements properly arranged and each listed with its abbreviation and atomic weight. He had shown his father the paper, saying, "Look, Dad, these are all the elements in the world." The father had been touched by the careful lettering and the neat enumeration of every element from hydrogen down to einsteinium and californium. Wanting to encourage the boy, he had asked if he would like to have a chemistry set. "Sure, Dad." He himself had had a chemistry set as a child. One of the experiments he had performed was the making of bluing. He could no longer remember what bluing was.

He had gotten Davey the chemistry set but it still sat in his room unopened, and the father realized that copying the periodic table had not been due to any intellectual curiosity, for the child had none, but had simply been an obsessive act. It was the sort of strange thing that Bart might also do in three years' time, except that Bart would not have placative motives. And he would not only never show his father his periodic table, but would probably shriek if anyone tried to look at it.

When they stepped out into the parking lot Davey said, "Boy, is this a one-horse town, huh, Dad!"

It was sunny and warm. Bart was standing shirtless by the

back door of the car, patiently waiting, dwarfed by the white-capped mountains. He was gazing down at the open catalog, the spine of which rested upon the slope of his jutting belly. He studied it, jam and syrup shining on his chin, as it rose and fell with his breathing.

Davey repeated, "This is a one-horse town, huh, Dad?"

The car was not locked, but one of Bart's peculiarities was that he would not climb into cars. The door had to be opened for him and he would then allow himself to be clumsily hoisted in, like an effigy of Prince Charles on its way to Madame Tussaud's. Tables, chairs, counters he would clamber onto, under, and around; anywhere but into a car. The father wondered at this, not for the first time. He felt a congestion in his chest. What was it about the boys? His anger swelled at them and at a world he was certain would make losers of both of them, the one a suck-ass, the other a mute. Why should disappointment be propagated through another generation, a cruel snap traveling down an endless rope?

"Dad, can we go camping again today? Drive back tomorrow?"

What did they want with him? Who were they?

"Dad?"

JOHNNIE GA-BOTZ

A telephone rings, filtered.

Both voices are filtered:

FIRST VOICE: Hello?

SECOND VOICE: Monk?

FIRST VOICE: Yeah.

SECOND VOICE: Johnnie.

MONK: Hey.

JOHNNIE: Okay, this is it, no more.

MONK: Hm.

JOHNNIE: Same bullshit, no money, whine whine whine.

MONK: Oh no. Okay.

JOHNNIE: Yeah.

MONK: So you want me to do it.

JOHNNIE: Yeah, now listen, this fuckin' guy, I want you, first I want you to cut off his dick.

MONK: Okay.

JOHNNIE: I want you to cut his fuckin' dick off.

MONK: Okay. I can do that.

JOHNNIE: And then I want you to stick it up his ass.

MONK: Whoa.

JOHNNIE: Yeah. Right up his fuckin' ass.

MONK: Whoa. His *own* cock?

JOHNNIE: Yeah his own cock, whose cock're we talkin' about?

MONK: Yeah, okay.

JOHNNIE: Fuckin' guy. Then you say, "Johnnie Ga-Botz wants to know how you like it."

MONK: Okay.

JOHNNIE: He says, ya know, I don't like it, you shoot him inna fuckin' head.

MONK: Okay.

JOHNNIE: Right inna fuckin' head.

MONK: Okay. Roger.

JOHNNIE: I don't think he'll like it, his dick cut off, stickin' up his own ass.

MONK: He won't like it.

JOHNNIE: But, ya know, he says he *does* like it, you still shoot him inna head.

MONK: Oh. Okay.

JOHNNIE: Whichever, ya know. You shoot him inna head.

MONK: Okay.

JOHNNIE: Or if he don't say *nothin'*, you shoot him inna head.

MONK: Okay.

JOHNNIE: Got it?

MONK: Yeah.

JOHNNIE: You cut his dick off, you stick it up his ass, "Johnnie Ga-Botz wants to know how you like it," you shoot him inna head.

MONK: Okay. So if . . . Well, okay.

JOHNNIE: What?

MONK: No no.

JOHNNIE: No; what?

MONK: Well, what if he—I know he says he don't like it, I shoot him inna head; he says he *does* like it, I shoot him inna head; he don't say *nothin'*, I shoot him inna head, okay I get all that, but what if he, you know . . .

JOHNNIE: What?

MONK: Well, says *some*thin', not I like it I don't like it, but somethin' *else*, so he's not sayin' *nothin'* . . .

JOHNNIE: What? So what?

MONK: Well . . . I still shoot him?

JOHNNIE: What the fuck? *Yeah* ya shoot him!

MONK: No matter what—

JOHNNIE: Ya shoot him—whatever the fuck!

MONK: Okay.

JOHNNIE: I don't give a shit what he says!

MONK: Right, okay.

JOHNNIE: The point is just—"Johnnie Ga-Botz wants to know how ya"—it's just so he'll know it was me.

MONK: Uh-huh.

JOHNNIE: Come on! Don't overthink this fuckin' thing! The point is to shoot him inna head!

MONK: Right.

JOHNNIE: The other stuff, cuttin' his dick off, stickin' it up his ass, that's just . . .

MONK: Extra.

JOHNNIE: That's just extra, that's just window dressing, what I *want* here is shot inna head.

MONK: I get ya.

JOHNNIE: Okay?

MONK: Yeah yeah, I get ya.

JOHNNIE: Fuckin' guy.

MONK: Yeah. Um . . .

JOHNNIE: Yeah?

MONK: I'm just . . .

JOHNNIE: Look, it's simple—

MONK: No, I understand it, it's just, I wanna consider all the—I mean at the time, I gotta know what to do if—ya know, I can't be callin' you with a question—

JOHNNIE: Yeah.

MONK: —while he's sittin' there with his, ya know—

JOHNNIE: Yeah.

MONK: —his dick up his ass.

JOHNNIE: Yeah, but it's—

MONK: I mean, "Johnnie Ga-Botz wants to know how you like it," that's so he—

JOHNNIE: So he knows it's me!

MONK: —so he knows it's you. But what if he's, ya know, passed out, loss of blood, whatever, the terror, ya know, the terror of his own dick up his ass—

JOHNNIE: Yeah.

MONK: So he don't know it's you, don't hear me sayin', "Johnnie Ga-Botz wants to know how ya like it," ya know, he don't know I'm gonna shoot him, he's passed out. He's out.

JOHNNIE: Yeah, okay.

MONK: What do I, I still shoot him?

JOHNNIE: Well shit, I don't, uh . . .

MONK: I still—

JOHNNIE: Yeah yeah, well try to bring him around, ya know, cold water, slaps.

MONK: Okay.

JOHNNIE: I mean *try*. And ya can ya can, and ya can't ya can't.

MONK: But I try.

JOHNNIE: Ya try.

MONK: Okay.

JOHNNIE: Okay. Ya got it all?

MONK: Okay. Lemme think. Okay.

JOHNNIE: The main thing is just—

MONK: Well the main thing is shot in the head.

JOHNNIE: Yeah, and the rest, as much as, ya know, circumstances, uh . . .

MONK: Okay. No problem.

JOHNNIE: Okay.

MONK: Okay.

Disconnect. Dial tone.

. . .

A ring, filtered, and an answering:

JOHNNIE: Hello.

MONK: Johnnie.

JOHNNIE: . . . Yeah. Whazzis.

MONK: It's Monk.

JOHNNIE: I know it's fuckin' Monk. You callin' me at home?

MONK: Yeah. Isn't that where you are?

JOHNNIE: . . . Yeah it's where I am, ya fuckin' called me here.

MONK: Yeah.

JOHNNIE: At *home*.

MONK: Oh yeah, yeah. But I hadda.

JOHNNIE: No you didn't hadda, what a you . . . All right, never mind, we're just chattin' here.

MONK: Yeah.

JOHNNIE: So, everything okay?

MONK: (hesitant) Yeah . . . yeah. It was fine. I did the first thing and, okay, he *did* pass out, but I slapped him around a little—

JOHNNIE: Whoa whoa whoa. What a you talkin' about—I'll call you. Don't—you at the place?

MONK: Yeah—no, back home, but the thing is, it was fine, he comes to, I do the other thing, you know, it's all done—

JOHNNIE: Whoa whoa whoa whoa whoa—

MONK: But now there're guys.

Beat.

JOHNNIE: Guys.

MONK: Yeah.

JOHNNIE: What guys.

MONK: Guys.

JOHNNIE: There?

MONK: No, here.

JOHNNIE: Yeah. There.

MONK: Not his place. *Here.*

JOHNNIE: Your place.

MONK: Yeah.

JOHNNIE: . . . *His* guys?

MONK: No.

JOHNNIE: Whuh . . .

MONK: Square guys.

JOHNNIE: There.

MONK: Mm-hm.

JOHNNIE: In the—in the room with you.

MONK: No, outside. Like parked across the, uh, I saw 'em when I pulled in. So I called you.

JOHNNIE: When?

MONK: Huh? *Now.*

JOHNNIE: *This* call.

MONK: Yeah.

JOHNNIE: Guys.

MONK: Yeah.

Beat.

MONK: . . . So what do I do?

JOHNNIE: . . . Well fuck. I, uh . . .

MONK: Ya know, uh . . .

JOHNNIE: Well first of all you don't call me at home.

MONK: Ah!

JOHNNIE: Huh?

MONK: They're knockin'. That's the door.

JOHNNIE: Fuck.

MONK: Ahh . . .

JOHNNIE: Fuck a duck.

There is the clunk of a receiver being set down.

JOHNNIE: Don't leave the line open!

Beat.

JOHNNIE: Monk!

Beat.

JOHNNIE: Son of a fuck!

Another filtered ring.

CHILD'S VOICE: . . . Hello?

JOHNNIE: Is Ed there.

The child does not reply but we hear a knock and thunk as the phone is set down. We hear the child distantly shouting:

CHILD: . . . Dad?

A long beat. We hear Johnnie breathing into the phone.

Finally, after a clunk:

VOICE: Hello.

JOHNNIE: Finn. It's me.

FINN: . . . Johnnie?

JOHNNIE: Yeah.

FINN: (sigh) Okay . . .

JOHNNIE: So what the fuck is goin' on.

FINN: Okay. First, ya know, I gotta tell ya, you're a fugitive, everything you tell me is privileged except your whereabouts, so if you tell me where you are I am not, uh . . .

JOHNNIE: Yeah yeah.

FINN: So bear in mind, uh . . . And I'm obliged to advise you to turn yourself in—

JOHNNIE: Yeah yeah yeah. What the fuck happened?

FINN: Okay. Well they got Monk.

JOHNNIE: Yeah, I fuckin' *heard* 'em gettin' Monk. How'd they know?

FINN: Well they were listening to your goddamn phone conversation. They hear him being sent out to whack a guy, they run over to Monk's place—

JOHNNIE: Yeah, but—

FINN: —they're waiting for him when he gets home.

JOHNNIE: Yeah, but how'd they hear the fuckin' call? I didn't *call* him at his place.

FINN: Where'd you call him?

JOHNNIE: His cousin.

FINN: . . . Georgie Mas?

JOHNNIE: Yeah.

FINN: Well *what the fuck*—

JOHNNIE: Georgie Mas is square!

FINN: Georgie Mas is a fuckin' punk! Georgie Mas is a fuckin'—listen, you don't wanna *know* what Georgie Mas is doin'!

JOHNNIE: *Georgie* Mas?

FINN: *Yeah.* Who *knows* why they might have a tap on Georgie Mas. Fuckin' . . .

JOHNNIE: Fuck.

FINN: (sighs) Well. Anyway. Obviously they *did* have a tap on him. And you call there.

JOHNNIE: Fuck.

FINN: So they hear you pushin' a button—uh, they hear what they construe is you soliciting, you know . . . soliciting Monk to . . .

JOHNNIE: Yeah.

FINN: Wipe a guy. So they go to Monk's house and wait for him to come home.

JOHNNIE: Uh-huh.

FINN: Gotta assume they got a wire on *your* phone, so they got Monk calling *you*.

JOHNNIE: Uh-huh.

FINN: We should fuckin' assume they got a wire on *this* phone.

JOHNNIE: (sigh) How can they tie me to that particular, uh . . .

FINN: Johnnie! You tell the guy to shove the guy's dick up his ass! Allegedly.

JOHNNIE: Uhh—

FINN: How many fuckin' homicides ya think they turned up that night with a dick up his ass!

Beat.

FINN: . . . I don't think we can be sayin', uh, it's a coincidence!

Beat.

FINN: . . . Johnnie?

JOHNNIE: Yeah.

FINN: So. Anyway. Monk's okay. He's not talking. I mean, to *me* he's talking, not to, uh . . .

JOHNNIE: Uh-huh.

FINN: But he's facin', ya know. You know what he's lookin' at.

JOHNNIE: Yeah.

FINN: Long fuckin' time. Circumstances—

JOHNNIE: Yeah, so forth—

FINN: —circumstances, so forth. *Long* time.

JOHNNIE: Yeah . . . Is my case, uh . . .

FINN: Johnnie, I'll be frank. I don't know what I could do for you. I don't, uh . . .

JOHNNIE: Yeah.

FINN: I don't yet see a strong defense.

JOHNNIE: Fuckin' . . . Okay. Well I'm in Barbados.

FINN: Huh? I didn't . . .

JOHNNIE: Yeah, it's okay.

FINN: I didn't catch that.

JOHNNIE: I'm in Barbados.

FINN: Well ya know, I'm obliged to, uh, pass that along, that information . . .

JOHNNIE: Whatever. I'm there.

FINN: So you're saying . . .

JOHNNIE: I'm in Barbados and I'll, uh, check in.

FINN: Okay. Okay. Fair enough.

JOHNNIE: Okay.

Click. Dial tone.

Filtered ring.

Two women, late middle age:

DOLLY: Hello?

JOYCE: Dolly?

DOLLY: Joyce?

JOYCE: Dolly. I'm sorry I haven't called—

DOLLY: No no, you poor thing.

JOYCE: Oh Dolly.

DOLLY: You poor poor thing.

JOYCE: Oh Dolly.

DOLLY: How's Johnnie.

JOYCE: He's very upset. The disruption.

DOLLY: Oh the disruption. It must be terrible.

JOYCE: He's not Superman!

DOLLY: It's terrible.

JOYCE: How long! How long!

DOLLY: Oh Joyce.

JOYCE: He can't come home, can't see the kids. Can't go out. He's gonna have a grandchild next month God willing. So—what? Life without grandchildren? Life in some apartment? Without grandchildren?

DOLLY: It's terrible.

JOYCE: I send him food, but . . .

DOLLY: Well that's good.

JOYCE: But reheated!

DOLLY: Oh.

JOYCE: I can't bring it to him myself. The police watch me. They know I would seek him with food.

DOLLY: Yes.

JOYCE: I give the food to Army. He takes it—he says it gets to Johnnie. Several handoffs. I ask will it reach him hot, he says no, he can reheat.

DOLLY: Ofer goodness . . .

JOYCE: This is not a life. Reheating? In an apartment? Never going out? What, cable television?!

DOLLY: Oh dear.

JOYCE: Is this a life?!

DOLLY: Tsk.

JOYCE: I say how long before I see Johnnie again? Army says, we don't know, it's not good, not real soon. I say when? When? Judgment Day?

DOLLY: It's terrible.

JOYCE: And he's two blocks away!

DOLLY: Oh my goodness.

JOYCE: He's hiding in Mario da Fina's apartment on Mott Street! Crazy! Two blocks away and I can't see him!

DOLLY: Oh Joyce.

JOYCE: The police would follow!

DOLLY: Tsk.

JOYCE: I go out to a public phone, I call him. He's very upset. He bellows.

DOLLY: Oh my.

JOYCE: I walk past One-twenty Mott Street I can't even look to the side. I can't go in. I can't call him from my own phone. I can't *talk* on my own phone! Not about him!

DOLLY: Tsk.

JOYCE: Right now I'm at Sarco's Egg Cream!

DOLLY: That's terrible.

JOYCE: Just to talk to you, from the phone!

DOLLY: This is terrible.

JOYCE: Cowering! This is a life? Cowering at Sarco's Egg Cream?

DOLLY: Tsk. Why don't you come over?

JOYCE: I'm shopping.

DOLLY: This evening.

JOYCE: This evening. Okay, I'll come over.

DOLLY: I'm so sorry.

JOYCE: It's my burden. What can we do?

DOLLY: What can we do.

JOYCE: (sigh) So how's your Georgie?

DOLLY: He's good.

JOYCE: Georgie's a good man.

DOLLY: He provides.

JOYCE: Georgie Mas is a good man. And *you'll* never have to worry.

DOLLY: Sometimes I worry.

JOYCE: Not things like *this*.

DOLLY: Sometimes I worry.

JOYCE: Georgie Mas? No.

DOLLY: Well. Maybe not.

JOYCE: I'll be over in an hour or so.

DOLLY: Okay.

JOYCE: Okay.

DOLLY: Bring me an egg cream.

JOYCE: Okay. What flavor.

DOLLY: Vanilla.

JOYCE: Okay. It'll be warm. I'll shop and come back.

DOLLY: Don't worry.

JOYCE: No, I'll shop and come back.

DOLLY: Okay.

JOYCE: Okay.

Click. Dial tone.

After a beat, a series of electronic clicks and beeps.

Silence.

I KILLED PHIL SHAPIRO

He was sitting in his office, eyes up to mine, his fingers at the adding machine frozen in mid-calculation. Calculus is Latin for pebble, stones having been used in reckoning. I pulled the trigger and his face burst apart, spattering the haroseth of his brains.

His office was at the end of an echoing limestone corridor in the Carmody-Wells Commercial Building. My walk there was straight and measured, like my walk to the bema when called on my bar mitzvah. Uncle Maury catered the bar mitzvah. He was a large shambling man with loose limbs, black hair all over his body, and glasses that swung from a strap round his neck. I have two other uncles who are also caterers, Marv and Yitzchak. But Uncle Maury submitted the lowest bid.

There were five brothers in my father's Bronx family. My father Phil and Uncle Schmuel were the only two who did not go into catering. My father was a fabric importer. Uncle Schmuel was a stillborn.

I killed Phil Shapiro.

He moved us to Minneapolis. I lived in that strange frozen city where people's breath hovers about them, where fingertips tingle and go dead, where spit snaps and freezes before it hits the ground. Finally I moved to the land of lawns of Harvard Law, and my nose stopped running. Harvard Law had for years been a topic in our house. Mother's friend Mimsy Kappelstein would always kvell about her boy, Danny, who had graduated sixth in his class. When I graduated fifth, Mother was already ill with the cancer that would kill her. She was in the hospital when she heard, being dripped. She strained to talk. Uncle Yitzchak leaned in close. Through cracked lips Mother whispered: "Tell Mimsy."

When I was little, the Kappelsteins were frequent visitors. Danny Kappelstein was very frum. We did not have separate dishes, milchig and fleishig, so whenever the Kappelsteins were coming for dinner we had to tell them what the meal was to be. If it was milchig, when the doorbell rang and Marty and Mimsy and Danny were waiting out on the stoop, Danny would be holding his blue-bordered milchig plate. If it was fleishig, he would be clutching his solid cream-colored fleishig plate. Milchig or fleishig, he wore his yarmulke.

One day it happened that Phil rather than Mother called the Kappelsteins with our menu. When they arrived—Marty, Mimsy, Danny home on summer vacation from Harvard Law clutching his blue-bordered plate, and Mimsy's father, Yikva, visiting from his old-age home in Toronto—Mother glared at Phil. We sat down to the table, Danny taking his usual spot before the vacant setting, where he put his milchig plate. When Mother came out with the pot roast, she said, still glaring at

Phil, "I guess we crossed signals. Danny may eat his roast directly from the pan."

Mimsy said, "My son will not eat from the pan like a savage Indian."

Yikva said, "Blintzes, nu?"

Mother said, "I will scramble Danny some eggs."

Danny's father blushed. "We thought it was blintzes."

Danny was staring down at his blue-bordered plate. He was six feet four and very skinny.

Mimsy said, "Danny had two eggs for breakfast."

Danny's father said, "That's all right. Danny likes eggs."

Mimsy said, "And the cholesterol? Four eggs in one day?"

Danny's father said, "So he'll skip his eggs tomorrow and it's even-steven."

Yikva said, "Blintzes, nu?"

Mimsy said, "And what'll he have for breakfast?"

Danny's father said, "He can have Wheatena."

Mimsy said, "We are out of Wheatena. I threw it out Passover."

Danny's father said, "And you didn't buy new?"

"I should buy new now that Mark is in Brandeis?"

"Danny eats it."

"Never."

"You eat Wheatena, don't you, Danny?"

"Danny eats eggs."

"So we'll pick up some Wheatena at Savemart on the way home and for one day he eats eggs. I mean Wheatena."

"Savemart is closed on the way home."

"Savemart is open till eight. Nightly."

"So we should finish by eight? We should bolt our pot roast like savage Indians?"

"Blintzes, nu?"

"Well then, he can have some of my Grape-Nuts."

"Danny doesn't have your stomach made of sheet metal."

"Grape-Nuts are extremely digestible."

"For *some* they are digestible. Barely."

"Well"—Danny's father shrugged—"he could skip breakfast one day."

Mimsy gasped. "A lunatic, this one."

Mother said, "I don't have to make him eggs. I could make him something else."

Mimsy said, "Danny, go to the kitchen and make yourself a peanut butter sandwich." She turned to my mother. "May we?"

"I'll make."

"Lots of peanut butter, not much jelly."

"Blintzes, nu?"

I killed Phil Shapiro.

This was not the first time that Phil had preyed upon gaunt Danny Kappelstein. A year earlier Mother had invited the Kappelsteins over for summer dinner on our porch. "Trail stew," Mother had told them, "like huntsmen eat." Mother's trail stew was overcooked carrots, soft and wrinkled peas, and stringy kosher cubed rump roast, with grease floating on top. I was the only one who saw Phil whispering something to Danny after dinner, just before Danny started vomiting. Of course I cannot be certain that Phil was telling him there was pork in the trail stew. I do know that Phil was smiling later, in the twilight, as he hosed down the patch of lawn where Danny had vomited.

Danny was a silent person. Later he married Deborah Goodman, who was beautiful. When they married, she shaved her head.

We went over to the Mensheviks' for dinner. Mike Menshevik said, "They invited me to China, there were no restrictions. I traveled where I pleased, talked to the people." He waved his cigar. "They are poor people, but they are smiling. I tell you this: I saw no misery in China." He had beard shadow on his dark face, shiny with oils. His belly bloomed over his belt. His wife, birdlike Dorothy Menshevik, had started dinner with a green ring-shaped jello mold. She made jello in a bundt pan. There was Del Monte fruit cocktail in it, and slices of old banana that bellied up to the surface like dead fish in an icehole. The main course was praches—cabbage stuffed with gray hamburger meat, studded with raisins—in a savory sauce. For dessert there was a yellow sponge cake shaped like the jello since it too was made in a bundt pan.

It was Mike's habit to go to the kitchen once or twice in the course of a meal; I had always wondered why. But this time I was fairly certain I heard a fart. The sound was muffled, yet sharp, as if Mike had cupped his hands over his buttocks, pressed himself back into a corner, and forced one out with a short violent hitch of his abdomen. I felt certain that this was what had happened and examined Mike Menshevik's face for a sign when he returned. But he only sat and resumed talking about China.

I killed Phil Shapiro.

Then there was Martin Brandeis, who farted aloud in Talmud Torah. These were not the furtive *shivarim* of a Mike Menshevik; these were *t'keyah g'dolahs*, proud shofar blasts that enraged his teachers and delighted us his classmates, except on muggy days. "Thunderbuns," we called him, and "The Eleventh Plague." When we were twelve, Martin confided in me that he wanted to become a rabbi and asked whether I thought he would make a good one. I was taken aback by his sensitive question. I pictured him farting up on the bema, but answered yes.

I remember another odor. I was on a train, carrying a brown paper bag. Inside were an egg salad sandwich on challah, wrapped in waxed paper, two tangerines, a banana with age spots, and a textured baggie containing mandelbrot. It had rained, and the smell of the wet brown paper mingled with the smell of the food. I felt sure that everyone could smell it and was wondering who on board had just visited his grandmother.

My grandfather then was already dead. I have a memory of him, visiting us. He sat in the armchair in the living room, his skin like the wimpled cover of an old siddur. "This fellow Wolff . . ." he would say, slowly raising one finger.

Grandmother hovered about him. "Abba, do you want a piece of sponge cake?"

I killed Phil Shapiro.

The evening that faraway Grandpa died: a phone call, Mother gasping, the rest of the evening quiet as Phil murmured into the phone. Mother sat at the kitchen table with one hand cupped to her forehead, drawing long, quavering breaths; on the stove a lid chattered over the stew.

Thus began the period where Grandpa ceased to be with us not because he lived in New York but because he was dead. Nevermore would he shuffle haltingly across the living room, touching furniture along the way.

Surprisingly, other people died. Both of Pete Diliberto's parents perished in a car crash, making an oddity of Pete. He was given a wide berth when he returned to school a few days later to stare shell-shocked at his desk. His return was brief; he went to live with relations in Michigan. Crashing a car was just the kind of stunt goys would pull. They had cheapened the whole death business. Grandpa, on the other hand, had done something quite natural, keeling over, as someone told me, of old age. I pictured him pausing between pieces of furniture and then tipping to the floor like a felled tree.

. . .

I want a snack. Mother gives me a nectarine with a soft dent in the skin. I look at it. Even without the dent, this is no snack.

Mother would place a weekly order with the kosher butcher for various roasts, pot and rump, and for the same gray ground round used in Dorothy Menshevik's praches. Out of this Mother would make either sweet-and-sour meat loaf or her hamburgers, which were dense gray spheres served on oversized egg rolls. As if it were a law of kashrut, we had rice when we had any form of beef, including hamburgers. The rice was served in the white waters in which it had simmered and which would gather at the center of the plate and sop into the hamburger roll. Mother would not drain it off, as it contained nutrients. For dessert we would have small friable chocolate chip cookies, dietetic ice cream, or macaroons.

Phil never complained about the food. He never talked at all. After dinner he would sit in his armchair in the living room and his cool blue eyes would rest upon the newspaper. He never asked me about school, or about Talmud Torah, except for a fleeting interest in Martin Brandeis when once I happened to mention his gift.

I was never asked if I wanted to go to Herzl Camp. It was a Zionist summer camp on the faraway shores of Lake Manitowish, Wisconsin. All I knew of it was its slogan: "If You Will It, It Is No Dream." I was brought to the Minneapolis Talmud Torah parking lot, where two chartered school buses sat idling;

each had a hand-lettered sign stuck to its windshield saying HERZL CAMP and beneath that (superfluously, I now think), "If You Will It, It Is No Dream." Cars were parked this way and that and trunks, doors, and hatchbacks stood open as duffel bags were unloaded and goodbyes bid. It was hot, crowded, and reeked of exhaust, and felt more like an embarkation of refugees than campers. Finally, its Zionist small fry stowed, the convoy pulled out. The two buses bounced on bad shocks through suburbs familiar to me, then unfamiliar, and then through countryside of stifling midsummer green. There were no formal stops, but whenever one bus pulled over the other did as well, to let a child disembark and vomit.

Upon reaching the camp there was processing. I remember a hot mowed field, clouds of gnats, and campers milling about with their duffel bags. The camp director, Rabbi Sam, was a dark slender man with a yarmulke and hairy legs and a tall gnarled intensity. He spoke a few words of welcome in which figured the phrase "If You Will It, It Is No Dream."

From the hot mowed field I went to a cabin, dark and cool. Bunk beds were ranged along the walls. I met those who were to be my comrades through six weeks of mandatory sports and prayer. We would swim in the lake, where I would press down on my trunks with both hands to force out gubbling air pockets. We would return to the hot mowed field, where we would slip stiff leather chafe guards over our fingers and shoot arrows at hay bales—an unpleasant activity which felt less like play than drill lest we be sitting ducks when the pogroms came to Wisconsin. In Arts & Crafts we would obediently make hideous creations of posterboard, glue, and uncooked macaroni. We prayed before eating, ate, prayed after eating, and then were allowed to sing Zionist songs as reward for having prayed, or perhaps for having eaten. We praised the Almighty far beyond what any reasonable entity would have felt comfortable with, and blessed many, many things.

Even so, we were spiritual slackers compared to those who attended the legendary Camp Ramah. That camp, in Rhinelander, Wisconsin, had an even more rigorous program of study and prayer and, according to rumor, no frivolities like our pontoon boat. We Herzl campers talked of Ramah attendees in low murmurs of respect, as we would of someone who had made aliyah. And indeed it seemed that the institution of summer camping was hierarchical, with Jewish day camps at the bottom, whence a progressive winnowing sent some onward to Herzl Camp, then Camp Ramah, and finally to the state of Israel. This I vaguely imagined as a great armed summer camp where it was indeed summer year-round and where people always wore Shabbas whites, slept in bunk beds, and made art of macaroni.

At the end of the six-week term we assembled again on the hot mowed field for the Sing-Away. During the Sing-Away the counselors, singing Zionist songs, would clap and stomp their feet in the center of a circle formed by we departing campers who, also clapping and singing, would run one lap around them and then up into the idling buses. What the goyishe bus drivers made of this I do not know. We pulled away; there was the shock of breaching the camp's perimeter for the first time in a month and a half, and then we made the oddly more and more familiar reverse drive home, to arrive back in the Minneapolis Talmud Torah parking lot as dusk gathered and our parents waited. It was as if the parents had been waiting the whole time and yet for an afternoon only, enjoying some perfectly ordinary tailgate party while we had punched a hole in space-time to explore a Zionist hernia of the Conifer Dimension.

Because my mother asked me and because the answer seemed as given as the answer to two plus two, I told her that I had enjoyed summer camp. Since I heard myself say it I myself believed it. I didn't have the words for how I really felt, and so how I really felt slipped away and returns to me now only in my fevers and dreams.

And finally, I remember Minda.

Max Minda was an elderly worshiper in our congregation. Between mutters as he dovened Mr. Minda would loudly hawk up phlegm. KHASHL would echo in the sanctuary over the murmur of prayer. After the service there would be a reception downstairs in Kapakin Hall. There would be pickled herring, sponge cake, and thick sweet wine. Sometimes there would also be gefilte fish in clear jelly, which Minda would eat with his fork chattering against the plate. Or he would stand in one corner, pushing sponge cake into his mouth with trembling fingers. There had been a Mrs. Minda, long ago. Minda's beagle face kept its secrets.

On my own bar mitzvah I blessed, praised, and gave immoderate thanks, and chanted my portion of the Torah wielding the yad, a tin pointer in the form of a small but meticulously modeled hand which to me seemed like a prop from Chiller Theater. After chanting my haftorah I bore the Torah itself around the congregation, leading the assembled in call-and-response prayer. I remember Minda, as I passed, leaning greedily out to kiss the Torah by means of his tsitsim. He fixed the same intent old-person's look upon the Torah as he would later fix upon the gefilte fish downstairs. He never looked at me. I might have been an orangutan ape who happened to be bearing scrolls.

There were medical men, also.

I remember the spitsuck sound of the oral evacuator. My mouth is puffed dry. I am in the operating chair at the office of Leonard Pink, Orthodonture. Dr. Pink finally pulls out the hooked sucking nozzle and the clumps of cotton that feel like mildewed mattresses in an abandoned lot. I salivate like a mad dog. He sprays my gums and teeth with water; a fine mist bounces back and I swish the water around and no longer have the mouth of a man four days dead.

I am twelve. In three years' time, my teeth may be straight.

Leonard Pink, a tall man with baby-fine white hair and bifocals, is in our congregation. Whenever Leonard Pink's name comes up Mother says that he is wonderful with children, but I have yet to see it. He works on my teeth in silence, and is soft-spoken and retiring with my mother and other adults. I suspect that he is a social imbecile. Weekdays he spends rooting around the mouths of adolescents, Shabbas he spends in shul, Sundays he plays cards with Harvey Colic the dermatologist while their wives, Roz and Shnee, walk around the lake. Shnee is a large woman with a forbidding bosom and flapping armflesh.

I see Dr. Colic also, for my acne. He is a loud, blustery man, quite unlike his retiring friend Pink. He has a red face and awkward tufts of red hair that fly like honking geese from either side of his head. When Dr. Colic notices a wart developing on my finger he bellows that I will have to attend WART clinic. He will not treat both acne and wart in one visit; he treats wart patients only on Tuesdays, at WART clinic. There is no practical reason for Dr. Colic to so consolidate wart patients; we are treated serially, not together, and the equipment is not elaborate—a simple hand-held wartburner that plugs into the wall. But, for the duration of the treatment of my fingerwart—it must be burned off gradually, over a period of weeks—I will have to visit him twice a week, once for ACNE, once for WART clinic. Dr. Colic seems to punch every mention of ACNE and WART, giving it volume even beyond his stentorian norm. More embarrassing, every Tuesday Dr. Colic tapes a hand-lettered sign to the outside of the office door—WART CLINIC—as if given to a medieval belief that we can be shamed out of our diseases of the skin.

So each Tuesday I sit in the wart waiting room with perhaps four or five other patients, each of us surreptitiously surveying the others for their warts. The age-veined linoleum, plastic-covered furniture, and the very pages of the unfresh magazines seem to harbor the diseases of patients long gone. When I am finally called in Dr. Colic removes my finger bandage and uses a slant-edge blade to scrape away the scaly white carapace that has developed, since my last visit, over my retreating wart. Then he applies the solder gun wartburner to the exposed raw wart. Dr. Colic hums loudly, turning my finger this way and that, and the office fills with the smell of burning wartflesh.

For a relatively healthy adolescent I spent a lot of time in the waiting rooms of various doctors. I know that most of the goyim with teeth and skin as bad as mine or worse saw neither orthodontist nor dermatologist, nor did they go to hogfaced allergist Fred Kiner who'd put his son, Larry, into military school. Mother said that Larry was a problem child. His problem, from what I could tell, was that he resembled Fred. Stout Fred Kiner always wore a stiff white medical tunic, buttoned at the side; when I pictured his child in military school I saw him wearing a similar shirt but with valor decorations, and a cap over his own little buzz cut, its brim pulled down over his beady little eyes. I saw him marching in place, one hand cupped under a riflestock, the other snapping a salute.

Dr. Kiner gave me various shots and monitored my various rashes, swellings, drips, and itches. As he absently examined me, depressed my tongue and peered into my throat, shone his little probe light into my eyes and then shoved it into each ear, flipped a loupe over his glasses and squinted at my skin, he would chat with Mother, who sat nearby on a straight-backed chair. Dr. Kiner would invariably stop short to examine a pustule and Mother would explain that it was not an allergic reaction but due to ACNE, for which I was seeing Harvey Colic. After a long discussion of my skin, studded with references to my pustule, Dr. Kiner would murmur, "How is Harvey?" and he and Mother would discuss Harvey Colic and then move on to Len Pink or Marty Blumenthal or Esther Gimple or Barry Zlotnick or perhaps Ed and Dora Glowicki whose eldest, Zack, was entering the rabbinate. Their conversation would continue as I put on my shirt and Dr. Kiner wrote out a new prescription and we went back out into the waiting room and Dr. Kiner leaned against the doorjamb and I put on my ski jacket and galoshes. As he and Mother chatted on I would stand there, hands thrust into my coat pockets, amid the waiting patients with various rashes, swellings, drips, and itches, human sumps and swamps who sat reading magazines.

When the conversation about the Glowickis had finally ended and Mother and I were outside, I would feel happily out of place. It was the middle of a school day and yet here I was in the parking lot of the Minnetonka Medical Park, across the street from the Golden Eagle Cleaners, with the sun beating down and the melting snow forming rivulets across the lot. There was the gurgle and drip of water falling from many icicles and the earthy spring smell of receding slush.

Perhaps Mother made me an aesthete by subjecting me to these never-ending torments. When, every week, Leonard Pink stuck a pair of metal pliers into my mouth and slowly and steadily twisted the wires that wrenched round my teeth; when I lay sweating on the tissue paper on Fred Kiner's examining table, a multijoint lamp glaring into my eyes and Fred squinting at me through his loupe as he manipulated a skin eruption with a small metal prod; when, in Talmud Torah, Mar Turchik bored us students into a nodding stupor but by means of intermittent questioning barred our escape into sleep; when at every meal I partook of our odd cuisine which tasted not like normal food but like belches after normal food—perhaps each moment of finely calibrated torture was a stimulus. My senses were never allowed to numb in the warm bath of pleasure. In every meal and Hebrew school class and doctor's waiting room I felt the pinprick of my differentness—from the goyim, the unreflecting, the free of wart. Perhaps the subtle torments bred fine appreciations. Our Passover Haggadah admonished me to act as if I personally, and not just my tribe, had been led out of Egypt. Perhaps this was Egypt.

And perhaps in his cryptic way my father was expressing the same thing. When I was eight Phil told me that Mount Rushmore was a natural formation. Wind erosion, he said. Nobody knew for certain how long it took or why it made those particular presidents. It was suspected that the mountain took its present shape at just about the time of the Christ. Phil was uncharacteristically voluble on the subject and said that there were geologists out combing the Rockies for more presidents and, indeed, for members of the legislature.

Several weeks later the subject came up in school, and after displaying my knowledge, I received the predictable ridicule. That's not what made me kill Phil Shapiro. But it is what made me suspect he'd told Danny Kappelstein there was pork in the trail stew.

It struck me in Hebrew school that God, the author of the Torah which was our only text, never lingers to dress the stage. Giants stand out against a featureless landscape. The very *chalav ood'vash* promised the Hebrews seems as abstract as the desert itself. And still the stories are sensual. The milk and honey may little resemble Dorothy Menshevik's praches, but then God was not writing for the fussy sensibility of our later age.

Sometimes the set decorations of my own life fall away to leave the bare limestone hallway of the Carmody-Wells Commercial Building. In my fancy, though, it is lit not by cold fluorescents but by torches held by slaves, each with his head cast down, eyes wrapped into an elbow. My echoing footsteps bring me past doors whose gilt lettering flickers in the torchlight—Leonard Pink, Harvey Colic, Mike Menshevik, Yikva of Toronto, Edward Glowicki & Son.

I pass these doors and go through the last one, unmarked. It lets out onto a windblown desert. Sand stings and drifts away, revealing huge monuments, fantastic animals made of stone. One in particular catches my eye: forelegs stuck out straight, hind legs curled beneath, wearing scrolled Egyptian headdress, its face in all its pocks and folds is that of . . . Max Minda. From the sand swirling around it a voice emerges, though the figure itself does not move.

Boychik, it says.

Hinayni, say I.

Takest thou thy father, thine only father, even Philip, whom thou lovest not, and make of him an offering.

How come? sayeth I.

The wind howls about the stone Minda and the great voice booms: So, smart guy, I need reasons all of a sudden?

The sandstorm dies; the graven Minda fades; the sun emerges. I smell the desert now, the rippled sand, the hunched fig tree, the earthenware jug in the well. The sun filters each smell through its dry heat and stamps each object with its hard light. Every thing is as sharp as a clap of the hand. Though I have never been here this landscape is familiar; I come from here; these desert sands and desert springs are more real to me than any place I've known.

A figure staggers toward me, arms limply dangling, linked footprints stretching back across the dunes. His white shirt glares in the noonday sun and his glasses are dusted with flour-fine sand. It is Phil—or given the fluid identity which dreams neglect to fix, it may be myself. I watch his approach and think about the proud Hebrew with dark skin and hook nose who once gazed out upon the many tents of his household. What connects me to him? Is the figure I now see the rear guard of a parade of ghosts, successive yet simultaneous, each generation melting into the next? What was passed down from father to son, even to the generation of Phil Shapiro, even unto our own day? What mysteries have been preserved, what lost, and what transformed in our migrations from Canaan to Eastern Europe to New York City and finally this far-flung garden suburb?

With vacant eyes the figure passes. The wind starts to fill the shuffling footprints he leaves behind even as he ascends a dune, stands swaying for a moment, and then lurches on, rippling, to disappear beyond the crest.

IT IS AN ANCIENT MARINER

Now it might interest you to know, stranger, that that barstool you are sitting on is the very one Radio Ronnie Harper was occupying when his wife bust through those doors and marched up to him and stabbed him in the neck, and both their little daughters watching. She had a Buck knife, Ronnie's own hunting knife in fact, and stuck it in wrongways. I don't mean handle first, how the hell you gonna do that, I mean cutting edge toward her, kind of sidearm, like she was boxing his ear. Except it was his neck. And that knife slides in like a good Buck knife will and she pulls toward her, which you're never supposed to do. You could get hurt. She was okay in this instance although Ronnie of course died of it.

No, I don't mind your sitting there, I'm just saying.

I myself was sitting right here, right next to him. This is my stool. No, thank you for asking, I was not injured. It was a domestic dispute, not a rampage. Ronnie's stool and mine, right next to each other. Here I sat and do sit now. Most folks still reference that as Ronnie Harper's stool. Only a year ago he died. No, nobody minds you sitting there. *We* don't do it as a rule, but not out of principle. Just prefer not to. So anybody sits there we know is a stranger. Well, not just because they sit there, but because we can see they're a stranger. If they weren't a stranger, they wouldn't sit there. Plus, we'd know who they were.

Thank you. Very kind of you. Seven-and-Seven.

What Ronnie did, worked for a manufacturing concern in town. Patterson Roofing Solutions. They make a, well, a kind of a goopus, has industrial applications. They spray it on a roof, it reflects back eighty percent of the sun's radiant energy. Beaumont Texas, you wanna get rid of that radiant energy. I don't know where you're from, but around here radiant energy is something we'd just as soon reflect right on back where it come from. Thank you anyway. Two kinds of places, one where they say, Well, but it's a dry heat, the other where they just say, Damn, it's hot. That's what Beaumont Texas is, just Damn, it's hot. . . . Well, okay, yes. I guess that *would* be a third kind of place, where it ain't hot in the first place. You're not from around here, are you. But that doesn't alter the point I'm making, which is that Beaumont Texas is a Damn-it's-hot kind of place.

So the way this stuff works is this goopus is got ceramic in it. It looks liquidy, but it's got microscopic ceramic particles in it, reflect the radiant energy. Plus it's white. Actually you can get different colors. If you don't want the white they can do you another color. Be a little less efficient than the white. Help, though.

Yeah, I did say industrial applications. Nobody puts it on their homes.

No, I don't know why they don't put it on their homes. I suppose they could. But you know, it's funny, most people sit where you're sitting, they're more interested in how Radio Ronnie come to get stabbed in the neck and his two little daughters watching, than in this goopy shit Patterson puts on factory roofs. I don't know why people don't use it on their goddamn house.

So Ronnie was a salesman for Patterson Roofing Solutions. Covered Beaumont, large part of East Texas, Port Arthur, even into Louisiana. Not a bad salesman. Liked. Respected, far as that goes. Drank here. Not to excess. Did drink, though. And that was his stool.

So he starts fornicating. How do I know? Well this is my barstool, and that you sit upon his. And he was dragging his sorry ass in here, getting sorrier by the day so I know something's wrong. And it's like he's just waiting for me to ask him so one day when his chin is down on the bartop I say Ronnie, and he says Uh-huh, and I say What is it.

And he says, I am one son of a bitch.

I say Yeah? He says Yeah, I been cheatin' on my wife. I am one lousy son of a bitch. Cheatin' on Alice, acting like a heel, fornicating with Marcia Ziegler.

Oh, says I. Marcia Ziegler also works for Patterson. Reception. Dark-haired woman. Scrawny. Surprised me, actually, that Ronnie was moved to fornicate with such a scrawny-assed individual. His wife Alice is very well proportioned. Two kids or not, she's a more attractive woman than Marcia Ziegler any day.

He says, Can you believe that shit, officer candidate? which is what we called each other sometimes from when we were in OCS though we both bag-assed out.

I say, Yeah, well, Jesus Ronnie, cut it out.

And he shakes his head and he says, I can't, man. I just can't.

Ronnie was an honest man. You'd look at him and you might think the opposite, just from how he dressed and being in sales and being easy with people like he was. See, he was pretty trim, my age—forty, both forty—and wore Tony Lama boots, lizard, pressed jeans, thin leather jacket nice and buttery. And of course his beard. Going a little to gray but always very neatly trimmed. Like he took a little too much care with it. So you figure, well he's a smoothy, but my point is no, he wasn't. Not at all. You sit on a barstool next to a man who's full of shit and pretty soon you'll know it. And Ronnie was foursquare, even *with* that beard.

Now Marcia Ziegler I happen to know. To say hello to, anyway. Scrawny-assed, as I had occasion to mention. With a way of talking that's a little snide. Like she can't say anything straight out, it's always got some dig or angle to it, always comes out the side of her mouth. Straight hair, bottom bob, hangs down like a little curtain her face peeks through. Ears stick out like a chipmunky animal. Don't know what Ronnie saw in her. Scrawny-assed.

I know that some of the other men she'd seen, eligible men, she'd pretty quick either dump or get dumped, either way saying snide things out of the corner of her mouth. Always talked like that. When she talks snide, if you take offense she'll laugh and say Just kidding out of the side of her mouth. Slip away at an angle, you can't talk to her head-on. Laughs a lot, Marcia, but just kind of heh-heh-heh; I never once heard her laugh like something actually struck her funny. Thin woman. Don't care for her.

Don't know that Ronnie did either, far as that goes. Not in the palsy-walsy sense. More just like BAM he had to nail that thing. I mean not just once, but keep bangin' on it. Missed days at the bar 'cause he was out nailing Marcia Ziegler. Went on a company trip once, this was some time after he confessed to me, Patterson organized a trip on the Nueces, canoeing, camping. Alice agrees Ronnie should go, have a little vacation from the girls—they had two little girls, Fonda and Annabelle, witnessed his death in the end although at this point they haven't yet, now he's just out canoeing—and Marcia Ziegler is on the trip as well. First night they beach the boats, make a camp, have a fish fry. Relaxing afterwards at the campfire and people said Ronnie gets all shifty-eyed and excuses himself. And they realize Marcia's gone too. Pretty soon from up in the woods they hear this caterwauling like a puma in heat, and Marcia's screaming, out and out screaming, "Fuck me Ronnie Harper! Fuck me Ronnie Harper!" Everyone at the fire sits there, they don't know where to look. Then the nervous laughs. And it keeps going, and they say it just got positively creepy, that screaming from out in the woods, like a wildcat over fresh kill. Creepy. Then, after a quiet spell, Ronnie saunters back to the fire, not with his chest thrown out like a high school kid bagged his first piece of ass, just shifty-eyed. Everybody tries not to look at him. And then Marcia waits what I guess she thinks is a decent interval which only makes it worse what with the suspense, and then *she* wanders back. Humming.

Well starting from then of course behind Ronnie's back

everybody calls him Fuck Me Ronnie Harper. Gets shortened to FM Ronnie Harper, then just Radio Ronnie. Folks figure that's obscure enough they start calling him Radio Ronnie to his face. I don't approve of that kind of thing, elbows and guffaws, but tell you the truth I don't think Ronnie even noticed.

See, he wasn't noticing much of anything around then. I mean, before that, you'd see Ronnie and he'd chat and be easy and free, but now Ronnie is always rushing away, kind of squirrelly, saying I'm late to meet a client but you always knew damn well who that client was. There was no joy in it, though, you could see that. It was this desperate look in his eyes like Ronnie was inside banging on the windows saying, Sorry, my dick is calling the shots now, but I'll get back with you as soon as my dick allows it.

See it was like Ronnie Harper was an appendage of his dick instead of the other way around. Like Marcia Ziegler had the world's most powerful damn electromagnet, like one of those junkyard babies can pick up a tractor-trailer and haul it across the lot, like she had one of those megawatt electromagnets right yango between her legs. And Ronnie Harper's dick just bypassed his higher functions, drug him around after, Ronnie bouncing along behind going Whoa shit Marie waving his arms for balance, like he's just hanging onto a towline and his dick the towline and Marcia Ziegler's privates a speedboat with an Evinrude one-twenty on it and Ronnie not so good a skier. It was like his penis—

Do you mind if I use the word penis?

It was like his penis—well hell, you might know what it's like yourself, you're about that age. Lots of guys when they get up towards forty, it's like their penis turns around and looks up and says, Hang on, hoss, you and me're taking one last ride before I pack it in for good. And it's off to the races. This was not about *liking* Marcia Ziegler. Are you kidding me? When you got a wife like Alice at home? This was a penis job, boy. Nothing but a damn penis job.

Now I— Thank you. Sure will. Thank you.

Now I haven't told you about Alice. This is where the story gets tragic. You might wanna think about having another drink here yourself.

Now Alice, she is a good woman. More than a good woman, a special woman. If Marcia is all sidelong angles and a bony little ass, then Alice is direct and straight and, you know, more womanly in her physique. You should've seen her in the little sundress she was in when she stabbed Ronnie. Very sweet. Blond girl. Freckles on her chest. And the tops of her arms there. Oh, you can see her in the little girls. Two blond little moptops. And how she doted on them. Positively doted. Man, you have not seen doting till you've seen Alice with her kids. Well, Ronnie too, far as that goes. You could not fault him there.

But Alice is like that with everyone. Loves people. Puts 'em at ease, right away, 'cause the minute you meet her you know you don't gotta watch your back. You're with friends. You're not with a salesman—though I ain't saying it wasn't genuine with Ronnie, the friendliness, hell, Ronnie liked people plenty, until his dick up and threw a shadow over it. But with Alice there was never any of that ambition shit mixed in. Just good feeling.

So what's a woman like that gonna do? Say, Okay, hell with my marriage, it didn't work out, I'll just start dating again?

Yes, Joe Bob, this *is* a lovely Chard'nay? Alice Harper? I don't think so, good buddy. This woman is too good for dates. Your Marcia Ziegler, your Marcia Ziegler, *she* dates. You take a Marcia Ziegler—

But this might be the time, here—maybe I should introduce a personal note. A little confession. Because, stranger, what'd I say before? Talking about Marcia Ziegler? Said I knew her to say hello? Well that's a half-truth there. Let me tell you something. I did not go all over town blabbing how I was a fornicator with Marcia Ziegler myself. Some of us just don't do that. We set back in the shadows a little bit, we're a little recessed. Laying back, there, in a covert fashion. Don't gotta go tell the damn world, but yes, I had known the lady myself. More than to say hello to. And let me tell you something. You want to know what it's like having sex with Marcia Ziegler you should do this: Go to the paint store—

Any paint store. It doesn't matter which damn paint store. There's a Sherwin-Williams over on Bowie.

Go to the paint store. Go in there, pull your pecker out, strap it into one of those paint shakers they got there and dial that baby up to Ten, or whatever the highest is. Jackhammer, whatever. San Francisco 1906. And while you're at it have one of the paint salesmen put his mouth right next to your ear and shriek, "Fuck me Whatever-the-Fuck-Your-Name-Is! Fuck Me Whatever-the-Fuck-Your-Name-Is!"

Nussbaum, huh? Hm. We don't get a lot of Nussbaums around here.

Well, anyway. Now you don't gotta sleep with Marcia Ziegler.

Very intense lady.

And did I mention, Nussbaum, that regardless of when you have your orgasm, you gotta leave your dick in that paint shaker for a good quarter hour?

Okay. Where was I.

So this is going on and it's common knowledge. So they're having fights at home, Ronnie and Alice, and finally Alice insists that the two of them go to The Healing Center.

The Healing Center, that's this ranch facility on the Guadalupe, over in the hill country, they have seminars and also one-on-one things, for personal growth. Also have wine tastings in the evening. So they're at The Healing Center for about a week. And Ronnie gets back, comes into the bar, sits on his stool—that one you're sitting on—and orders a beer. And he has a black eye the size of a plum.

So I just play stupid, I say, How was it, Ronnie? How was The Healing Center?

And he looks down at his beer kind of shifty-eyed, and his arm stretching forward makes his leather jacket ride up past his chin, he nods down at his beer and says, Not bad. Nice place. Spectacular setting.

And everyone comes into the bar looks at him and asks him how was it and he nods and says, Spectacular setting.

And he looks like a man under sentence of death, the strain still there in his eyes. Because he was a prisoner. The man was a prisoner of sex.

Thank you. No, maybe I'll switch to a Bombay martini here. Red Dog back. Thank you.

But I was telling you about Alice. This is a good woman.

This is a woman—how do I describe it. When you go to the store to buy a cantaloupe and you want to see if it's ripe, you heft it and give it a little thump, and if it sounds nice and plunky then you know it's a good goddamn cantaloupe. Well that's Alice's ass. Not that Alice had a fat ass—not at all. No, it was just right, made you want to thunk a knuckle against it to hear that perfect sound. Not like Marcia Ziegler's scrawny little ass.

And having sex with Alice was like swimming on the sweet rolling sea. Like the tide pulling you in. Bringing you safely home. Not like Marcia Ziegler, yanking you home like a bad dog. Where you run a danger of whiplash. I swear, sex with Marcia Ziegler, it feels like she's got wires crossed in her ass. And her orgasm is like a pinball machine ringing up your eight hundred thousand bonus points. Chinka-chinka-chinka-THWOCK-chinka-THWOCK—you know what I'm saying. And then she'll just lie there a moment to catch her breath and then go "Huh!" Just "Huh!"—like the bonus ball burping up.

But Alice—with Alice, it's smooth and sweet and free. Because she's a *woman*, Nussbaum, y'understand. Wrapping you up and holding you with her love, but giving herself, sharing, sharing cries of joy, Nussbaum, that are almost unbelievable, like in a church pew, a goddamn *pew*, Nussbaum, or when you gaze upon some scenic beauty so goddamn fresh and high it is almost beyond your power to take in. Your heart can't take any more, it must give forth, it must share its joy with her, so that her heart will pound with the same joy, the joy she draws from *your* pounding heart. It is that kind of deep, *deep* giving and loving and sucking and fucking and fucking and sucking and sucking and fucking. And afterwards, not that damn businesslike "Huh!" Afterwards—weeping.

And sweetness. *Bitter*sweetness, Nussbaum. Dripping, weeping, sighs. I am not a weeping man, Nussbaum. But the *world* weeps. You lie there and the world is a great weeping bayou, and Alice and you are on this bed which is now a pirogue floating off into the twilight as a distant bird cries—

A boat, Nussbaum. A pirogue is a kind of a boat.

No, it's not clammy. I'm not talking about the goddamn sheets being wet. The dripping is not a literal thing. It's a feeling. Jesus Christ, you got a goddamn narrow little mind there, Nussbaum, I don't care how many drinks you buy. I'm talking about people's souls, and you're talking about jiz dripping on the sheets. Grow up, man. Show a little maturity. Jesus Christ.

Yeah, okay. That's okay. Yeah, forget it. Thanks, man. The same. Yeah. Beer back.

Now this is why it was sad. This is how come it's so goddamn sad, Nussbaum. I mean, you look at pictures of them when they were kids, Ronnie and Alice. They were high school sweethearts; I don't believe she'd ever had another man. And there's the two of them, Ronnie beaming at the camera, Alice with her arm hooked around his, beaming up at him. Beaming at him. Like he has the only penis in the world. So goddamnit amighty, ain't it lucky she found him. And the future, ain't no future on their minds—hell, ain't gonna be no problems there, ain't even worth thinking about. What the hell, he's *got* the penis. Grinning, and if he's grinning, well then why wouldn't Alice grin too. Kids. What do kids know. What do kids know, Nussbaum.

Yeah, no, I meant she'd never had another man *then*. When they got together. Or afterwards either, for that matter, up until Ronnie started in with the hankie-pankie. And even then it wasn't spite. Wasn't tit for tat, Alice wasn't sleeping with me to get *even*. She's not that kind of woman, Naumbus, she didn't even think of it as having sex. Nussbaum. Sorry. She just had to unburden herself. She had to share, share with someone; it was reaching out. She reached out. This is a sweet woman. And her husband says, he's saying, "Our sex life is blah." That's what Ronnie said. At The Healing Center. In front of a counselor. And then he suggested they use *sex toys*? A woman like Alice—*sex toys*? Alice Harper will not use dildos, Nussbaum. Not for you, not for me. Not for this man's army. Dildos are out of the question. "Our sex life is blah," he is saying, in front of a guy with a ponytail. A nodding guy with a ponytail. And dildos. This incredible, incredible woman. So she reaches out—

It is *not* the same thing. That is just ignorant, and just shows that you haven't understood what I been telling you about each of these people. *He* did it, 'cause he was a damn sex fiend. He couldn't control himself. It's not that *she* couldn't control herself.

Yeah, she stabbed him. But she—she—okay, in that sense she couldn't control herself. But that's not—that doesn't make her, uh . . . Her and Ronnie, it was love. Sometimes it comes from a place of love. A place of love, Nussbaum. Don't you goddamn understand that?

Well that's because you don't understand love.

No, but—

No. No you don't. Not if you say, "She was fucking someone

too." You don't understand *shit*. And you're goddamn *right* I was his best friend. So get the fuck off that stool. Right the fuck now. Asshole.

No, I will *not* answer one question. Just get the ffffff—

Huh?

Marcia? No.

No, I don't know whether she's currently dating.

GATES OF EDEN

I pulled into the self-serve island of Herve's on Highland, up to where it meets the freeway. I got out my two five-gallon provers. I put the regular nozzle into the red prover and squeezed. When the pump read five gallons, the bottom of the meniscus rested on 4.59. Herve was coming out to watch, wiping his hands on an oily rag.

I started gassing up the green one, this time unleaded.

"Looks bad, Herve." The pump was humming away, a happy little bandit.

"I had those pumps fixed, man."

"I should hope so, Herve. I gave you three months." We both watched the numbers climbing on the pump. "But the regular sure did look bad."

He looked at the can and licked his lips. "I got those suckers fixed."

The pump was turning over to four gallons, but the gas in my state-issue can was bubbling short of its four. "The unleaded don't look so hot either."

I was easing off on the pump. One more squirt.

The pump read five State-of-California gallons.

The meniscus read 4.41.

Herve paled. "I don't understand."

"You don't understand." I holstered the nozzle, affecting calm. "Well, let me try to explain." When I wheeled, my right fist caught his throat.

He dropped, clutching at his Adam's apple and trying to suck air.

"I told you three months ago. Calibrate these sons of bitches!" I kicked him twice. "Don't fuck with the public!" He was still scrabbling at his throat, turning the mottled red of an L.A. sunset. "The meniscus don't lie, greaseball! Read the state manual!" I bounced a copy of the four-hundred-page book off his ear. "It'll tell you everything you need to know!"

I grabbed a tire iron.

Herve was moaning, trying to crawl away with one hand clawing at the pavement, the other pressed to his inflamed left ear. "That green card you got ain't a license to steal." I hefted the tire iron. "This is your second warning," I bellowed. "The state don't give three!"

I spun, around and around and around, and let go the tire iron. There was a crack like a pistol shot and the plate glass front of Herve's went away.

I tossed the provies into my car and took off.

My name is Joe Gendreau. California Weights and Measures.

. . .

Our bureau works out of an avocado-colored bunker in Hollywood. It isn't much, but then I don't have clients to impress. My duty is to the public—not that they ever thank me. Your average consumer doesn't know that I'm the only thing standing between him and chaos.

Standards are what make us a society. A community agrees. A gallon is a gallon. A pound is a pound. He who says fifteen ounces is a pound—he must be put down. A pound is a pound, or we go bango.

I hate a gyp. I hate it more than anything. The man who laughs at standards—that man must be put down. We are none of us perfect; I know that. But we must agree on what perfection is. I thought I'd met the perfect woman once. I was wrong, yes. Terribly wrong. But still.

There was a knot of idlers laughing around Marty Shechter's desk, as usual. He was doing his Charles Nelson Reilly impression. Marty is a skillful operative, but he lacks commitment. For a lawn party—sure, ask Marty Shechter. For a job of work—no. Or rather, for a job of work—yes, Marty Shechter, provided there's no one around for him to showboat to. That's how I feel about Marty Shechter.

On my desk were messages from two gypmeisters who were contesting. I would have to make court appearances. And then there was a new complaint, from a Miss O'Hara, a colleen with a West Side number. Ordinarily I call to make an appointment for an interview, but her line was busy and, what the hell, she'd left her address.

. . .

I knocked at the door of a big sort of ranch house up Brentwood way. The Jap maid who opened the door was got up in native dress. She was young, and pretty in that dolly way of theirs.

"Hiya, sweets." I swept my hat off my head and grinned. "I'm here to see Miss O'Hara."

She exploded into tittering laughter, like the sound stars would make if they bounced off one another like wind chimes—or for that matter, like the sound of wind chimes.

I wasn't in on the okejay, but her girly little laugh made me not mind. I did a fast soft-shoe and kidded back: "Tell her it's Fred Astaire."

She tittered some more, her hands flying to cover her cute little dolly mouth, her knees punching at the front of her kimono. "Missa Astaire," she finally gibbered, laying to rest my fear that she didn't savvy the English. "Name not a O'Hara. Ohara. I Ohara. I a house a head a house a."

It took a moment for me to decode it, that she was the mistress and not the maid. She tittered and bounced around some more, getting quite a kick out of watching my face drippin' egg.

I kicked at the stoop and mumbled, "I'm terribly sorry, Miss Ohara. I guess my message—I thought it was from a—well, never mind. But my name isn't really Fred Astaire—it's Gendreau, Joe Gendreau. California Weights and Measures." I fished out my buzzer and gave it the copflip. "I hope you'll excuse the misunderstanding."

"A Missa Gendreau." She was still giggling in her girlish, dolly way. "Come in a talk."

I did go in. The place was pleasant like I somehow knew it would be, with clean gleaming wood and paper-paned partitions. It felt all open and airy, like a Jap restaurant but without that plinky-plink music.

Her little dolly head bounced in front of me as she led with a mincing walk, hands gathering the kimono in front. I reflected on how she hadn't been offended by my little gaffe, whereas her Western sister would undoubtedly have pitched a mood. Well, that's the beauty of the Eastern female. We might tag her submissive or unliberated or what have you, but to my mind she has a grace and dignity all her own, bred by centuries of tradition. Her purpose in life, which she will ever strive to perfect, is the serving of her master, Jap though he may be.

We were entering a little area with a low wood dining table set out for two.

"We eat a fuss."

"I appreciate the offer, Miss Ohara, but I really couldn't impose. Whatever I can help you with, if you'll just—"

"We eat a fuss. Fussa we eat."

She bowed and grinned, not giving an inch. Departmental regs have things to say about chumming up with complainants, but they don't tell you to be rude either, and the woman had it in her head that we were going to eat.

I sat down on the floor, as chairs there were none. Little Miss Ohara, still grinning, slipped off my shoes and briefly rubbed my feet. I was embarrassed, but if she was aware of any foot odor, she didn't let on. She poured something from a little crockery doodad into the little crockery cup in front of me, then went away chirping. I reached for the cup and smelled. Sake. I tossed it back. Nice stuff, sake. Easy going down.

The little duchess was trotting back in with a lacquered board upon which were various fishments and wrapped textured tidbits, laid out with plenty of grace and charm, like a little garden. I marveled at the grace and charm.

She knelt before me, giggling, holding the board above her bowed head.

"Thanks, Miss Ohara, but why don't you sit down also and—"

"You eat a. Man muss eat a."

I shrugged and popped one of the morsels in the old bocarino. It was tasty, delicate. I reached for more. My fingers felt big and clumsy on the cool daintiness of the food. "You finis," she said, setting the platter in front of me. She poured some more sake and bounced to her feet. As she did so, I couldn't help noticing some chestiness where her kimono hung momentarily open. I knocked back more sake, dancing in hob boots on departmental regs. What the hell. Some bureaucrat sitting in an office in Sacramento can't possibly anticipate all the situations faced by the man in the field.

The little contessa had skipped out of sight, into the living room. "Miss Ohara," I called after her, "I sure do appreciate the hospitality, and you have a beautiful house and whatnot. But if we could just get down to cases here, we—"

I heard humming and, naked as a jaybird, she flitted across the wedge of living room open to my view. She did it in a dancing, carefree kind of motion, her arms held out at her sides, Zorba-like, with a faraway smile on her face.

It was the damnedest thing.

I sat quietly, watching, hoping, I guess, that she would Zorba back the other way.

Well, no such luck. She reappeared, after a minute, in a different kimono, tightening the sash. I guessed it was the after-lunch job, maybe for the tea ceremony. Once again I tried to put across the theme of my business:

"Hello again, Miss Ohara. I gather you know that I'm responding to a call you made to Weights and Measures. I—"

"Come look a garden," she said, and spun on her heel.

What the hell; I was done arguing.

The garden was—well, it was nice. A nice little flagstone path led through nice beds tiered with flagstones. Some of the beds were dirt; some were crushed white rock. It was a hell of a collection of greens and flowers and little trees, but not all gaudy and overstated like some gardens you see. No, somehow it was all just right, just like lunch had been, all sort of pleasant, with a lot of thought behind it, careful thought. Somewhere I heard a fountain gurgle. Yes sir. It was one hell of a thoughtful arrangement.

The princess was leading me with her little mincing step, like a champion show horse. My feet were landing harder than hers—that's the thing with sake, it goes down so smooth you can forget how much you've drunk. The path rounded some low shrubbery and ended in flagstone steps leading down to a little rock pool. The eucalyptus trees rustled in a light breeze, and somewhere bees droned. I was feeling pretty damn good.

I stood there swaying. I watched Miss Ohara's shoulders work as she tugged at her clothing. Her broad satin sash fell away to either side, and when she gave a little shrug, her kimono slipped off her porcelain shoulders onto the ground. She was a naked little dolly. She stepped daintily into the rock pool, like some delicate creature slipping into a mountain lake to perform its natural bathing activities. When her steps cut the water, there was barely a splash.

I loosened my tie. The garden was fat with life, like a drowsy bumblebee on a scented summer day. But this man-made garden was more beautiful even than nature; it was perfectly composed, as if civilization at its highest had fused with nature, and each had made the other something higher still. I seemed in that moment to understand what Miss Ohara was trying to tell me, that she too was part of this nature, moving in oneness with the water, rolling in it and letting it roll over her. There was no shame in the garden, only beauty, beauty not just to look upon but to join in and be one with. Human beauty, natural beauty. I too could be beautiful. I could be part of the garden, perfect, just as she was. We could be man and woman, in the garden, without words, without shame. We could abide in beauty and be one.

With thick fingers I pulled off my tie, my banal tie. I pulled on my shirt buttons. It was slow going; I ripped the last few away and tossed the shirt. I sat to take off my stockings; they were too tight; I pushed hard, got my fingers jammed up, finally got them off. Back on my feet I unbuckled my belt, dropped my trousers, then stepped out of my shorts and was free. I was free in the garden. The warmth of the sun bathed my shoulders. A breeze played across my privates and made the eucalyptus rustle. Somewhere, far away, bees droned on.

Miss Ohara swam lazily, unselfconsciously corkscrewing through the water. The water pushed unbroken over her body like a stream slipping over a smooth stone. I stepped into the pool.

The sun had warmed the water. Its warmth drew me in, tickling my flesh and drawing my weight away. As I immersed myself, I was as light and graceful as Miss Ohara, a creature of the water. She laughed and pushed her body toward mine. "Fussa *yaw* needs." My privates had become swollen, enormous, not from lust, as you or I know it, but as an expression of nature. Miss Ohara treated it not with dirty shame but with joyous love. "Help me, Miss Ohara." She smiled, and gasped a little when we first achieved oneness. The extent of my love surprised her; I guess they don't grow as big as mine in the shadows of Fujiyama. But then she moved with me in the shallows of the pool, and we obeyed the command of the garden. Our bodies swayed in the waves that we created. We were carried along by each other and by the gently rocking pool, and we performed the ancient act.

I opened my eyes.

I was lying facedown on the flagstones near the pool. My feet trailed into the water. The water was cold. The wind stirring the eucalyptus was chill now, and the garden gray. It was evening.

I was a beached whale. My body ached from its own weight on the flagstones. Shivering, I struggled to my knees. The flagstones dug into my knees; I pushed myself to my feet. The movement made my eyes pound and roused sumo wrestlers who blundered inside my head, slapping bellies, their weight tilting this way and that. As I looked for my clothes, my head swam about, adjusting late for the wrestlers' trundling inertia. I realized how I must look, and cupped my hands over my privates.

"Miss Ohara?"

The wind made rustling noises in the trees. There was no other sound.

I pressed my hands against my head to stop its swaying. I saw my clothes nearby, where I'd dropped them. But stooping for them squeezed my stomach, which squirted acid into my throat. I tried by force of will to calm my leaping stomach, and clamped my eyes shut as I stepped into my shorts. I straightened slowly, but not slowly enough. The wrestlers were back into their stagger, my head swimming with them.

Things spun dizzily. The flesh on my back was tingling, yet numb. When I squinted down at my shoulder, it seemed far away, as if I were a giant looking down on someone else's body. The flesh was very red. I pressed thick fingers into it. It turned ghastly white around my fingers, then quickly red again when I stopped pressing. My chest and stomach were still pale, marked by flagstone ridges. My penis was small and gray.

My back had been roasting in the sun. That, and the alcohol, explained the dizziness. But what was the terrible ache thumping in my buttocks? I pushed my shorts gingerly back down and reached back with both hands. As I lightly grazed my buttock region, the pulsing ache exploded into white-hot pain. My posterior was swollen and inflamed, skin stretched tight over irregular bumps, as if someone had sewn roasting chestnuts into the flesh. I remembered the drone of bees, now silent. That was it. Bee stings.

"Miss Ohara?"

Only the wind.

As I withdrew my hands, the stinging lapsed back into a throb. But the pain had reawakened my nausea, and now something else stirred deep within my bowel. I knew the feeling. Pressure dark and deep, it was the herald of an approaching stool. I tightened my buttocks. This recalled the stinging buttock pain, but I needed to contain myself until I could dress and find a bathroom.

I aimed one foot at a leg hole in my trousers, thrust desperately, missed. My hands shook with the rumble of approaching freight. I shouted at myself, words of calm, and guided my foot into the hole. The pressure was unbearable. My sphincter quaked with the effort of staying shut. I hopped into the second pants leg, convulsively clutching my buttocks against the onrushing tide. No longer rhythmic, it swelled only, without ebb. The pressure set my body shaking—I was not going to make it. This was it; there was no denying the clamor at the gate, beating, pounding, frantically rattling the latch—this was it. I kicked away my pants and was dropping my shorts when the thing was upon me. I could only hunch forward, knuckles of one hand on the flagstone, buttocks thrust out behind me, in the three-point stance of the scrimmage line.

It came splushing out all liquidy and with a lot of fanfare, if you catch my meaning. There was no containing it, no way to let out just enough to ease the pressure. It blew, but good.

It had been cooked into a thin paste by bee poison and sun. Most of it blew back, but as it petered out, some dribbled onto my shorts and calves and ankles.

It smelled as if it belonged to someone else.

After the last of it had sputtered out, I stayed crouched, frozen there, for several moments, my sphincter quivering. I hunched there, hot yet cold, flushed yet clammy, until I became aware of my knuckles aching against the stone. I straightened up. I stepped out of my spattered shorts and turned round, trembling, to survey the damage.

My feces were all over the garden. They flecked the entire flagstone area. Some had even reached the bordering flower bed. They were a dark brown-black.

The expulsion had left me feeling weak and dizzy, dizzy and weak.

"Miss Ohara?"

Only the tree-rustling wind.

My buttock cheeks were slick against each other. I had to tidy myself.

I picked up my soiled shorts and, holding them out away from my body, waded into the pool. The water was cold now; as it crept up, it pushed out gooseflesh and made my skin feel heavy and dead. When it reached my thighs, I paused, sucked in my breath, and did a fast knee bend. The ice water slapped at my anus, igniting the bee stings, and sloshed angrily around my testicles. I did several more knee bends, then staggered, shivering, out of the pool.

I realized that I was no longer holding my shorts. I looked back at the pool. There they were, floating away like a lily pad in the failing light, a charcoal smudge on dull linen paper.

I stood there for a moment, trembling in the breeze. I picked up my trousers. Their texture, as I began hopping in, seemed terribly rough. I looked at my penis, and forced myself to look away. Still shriveled and gray, it had looked like a dead man's.

Miss Ohara's house was locked and dark; I left the garden by a side gate. I won't bore you with the details of how I managed to drive home. Leave it at this: that I was cold and hurting, and the whole way back I wept with shame.

That night I lay on my stomach, thinking, with a fan aimed at my buttocks smeared with salve.

What did it mean?

When I got to work the next morning Marty Shechter was doing his Paul Lynde. People were laughing. I went into my office and dialed the number I had for Miss Ohara.

No answer.

I drove the streets, a doughnut cushion on the driver's seat. I was sapped, listless, still weak from sunburn and the purge.

Over on Van Nuys I walked into a Happy Burger and ordered one. The bald black counterman said, "Deluxe?"

"What?"

"Fries widdat?"

"No."

"Bevidge?"

"Just the burger."

He stooped to open a minifridge facing the counter and raised his voice over the grill fan: "How do you want it, medium?"

"Raw."

"You huh?"

"Raw."

Slowly he straightened, eyes on me, holding a papered patty. "Real rare, huh?"

"Raw," I said for the third time. "And never mind the bun."

He looked at me, then down at the patty. Slowly, sadly, he slapped the patty facedown onto the plate. His hand came away with the paper backing. He shuffled reluctantly toward me, staring at the plate; when he reached my stool, he stopped but didn't put it down. He stood motionless, frowning at the plate, feeling the distress that any good counterman would feel on serving a naked patty.

At length he mumbled, "I put it on a bed of lettuce," and started to turn away.

I grabbed one elbow, snarling, "Give it here." He watched as I opened my kit and took out the scale. "Who owns the place?"

"Huh?"

"Who's the boss?"

"Mistuh Katz."

"He have a first name?" The burger weighed in at just under 6¼ ounces.

"I guess."

"This *is* Happy Burger, Home of the Seven-Ounce Bun-Buster?"

"I guess."

"You don't seem sure of much."

"I don't get paid but for knowin' how to cook."

I flipped him my card. "Tell your boss to call if he wants the padlock taken off the door."

I drove past the house in Brentwood, staring like a lovesick schoolboy. I thought of ringing the bell but couldn't picture what would come next. Where would we begin? *Could* we begin again? Could I ever explain the mess in her garden?

The whole thing—had it even been real?

An eight-by-ten envelope was on my desk. It had been hand delivered. On its face was handwritten my name and, underneath, the word "PERSONAL."

Somehow, I knew.

I closed the door to my office, put the doughnut on my chair, and stared at the envelope for a long moment before I opened it.

They say that pictures don't lie. Well then, I guess I

dreamed all of what happened between me and Miss Ohara. These pictures didn't show a man and woman celebrating their oneness. They showed a sagging middle-aged guy screwing a Jap. Shame, shame—all I felt on looking at those pictures was dirty shame, shame that Miss Ohara had seen me naked. I mean, hell, she looked pretty damn good. And I was—well, if I just had a month or so to work out a little, get back in fighting trim. . . .

But there were more than just the action shots. There were a couple of front angles of me with Miss Ohara, later stuff I didn't remember. She'd wrestled one of my arms over her shoulder and had me lolling in the pool next to her. Her gaze was cool and businesslike; I was grinning like Crazy Guggenheim. Jesus, I needed a brassiere worse than she did. Anyway, after these posed shots—meant to leave no doubt that it was me with the naked little missy—there was a picture that showed what had happened before I woke up. I was sprawled out facedown on the flagstones, mouth gaping like a fresh haddock's. Miss Ohara, in a kimono now, was squatting over me, along with a Jap guy in rimless glasses. Miss Ohara was holding a jar open-end down against my buttocks. The guy was tapping at the jar. The picture wasn't so sharp that I could see the activity inside the jar, but of course I knew.

Well, that was it. There weren't any pictures of my last adventure in the garden, the one I remembered all too well. They had probably left long before I woke up. As message there was only a slip of paper bearing an awkward scrawl: "LAY OFF A YATSIMURA BROS."

Jimmy Yatsimura and his brother, Wa, ran a fruit stand in Santa Monica. I'd been looking into them since their scales never seemed to match their customers'. But so far, somehow, they'd spotted the DWM shoppers and we hadn't been able to nail them.

The message was clear. If I didn't toe the line, these gyp artists would show the pictures to my boss, to the public at large, to whomever. Except for the last picture, the one with Jimmy Yats. They'd just thrown that in to twist the knife, so I'd know how the bee stings got there, that it wasn't just happenstance. It got my goat, all right—not just the pointless spite but the planning that must have gone into the whole thing. The act with Miss Ohara, whoever she was (Ohara probably being Nipponese for Joe Doakes or what have you). The mickey finn in the sake. Hell, maybe they'd also slipped in some kind of Tokyo depth charge to shake up my bowel. I slowly flipped through the pictures, again and again, at the end of every cycle coming to the slip of paper—"LAY OFF A YATSIMURA BROS." I looked at them, at her, at myself. Again and again. Dirty shame. Again and again.

I don't know what I was thinking when I drove out to Santa Monica that evening. I hadn't planned anything. I was just going there. There was no plan. I was still in a daze. There was no plan.

I walked into the fruit stand and browsed along the table of iced lettuces. I thought, What the hell are all these different lettuces? Did the Japs bring them? The Koreans? Why did they bring so many? What kind of society has ours become, when one kind of lettuce is no longer enough? Isn't the need for variety, past a certain point, a sign of decadence? Why do we need to be teased with subtle flavorings and exotic strains? The kind of person who needs that much variety in his sex life, we call a pervert. The true man, who is hungry, eats.

The true man eats.

I ripped a plastic bag off the plastic bag roll and started dropping in navel oranges. When the bag was full, I ripped off another bag and filled it. I brought the two bags over to the register and put them down on the counter. "Two bags of navel oranges, please," I said.

Behind the counter, Jimmy Yatsimura picked up the bags and put them on his scale. He gave no sign of recognizing me. He punched in the price per pound and waited for the numbers to settle.

I looked at him looking at the scale. He stared through his rimless glasses, his tongue stuck between his teeth. I wondered if he was having a sex relationship with Miss Ohara. I felt certain that he was. I tried to picture it, Jimmy Yats and Miss Ohara. I wondered if they did it in the garden. I felt certain that they did. I could see him clearly, engaged in the act, wearing nothing but his Mr. Moto glasses, his tongue sticking out between his buckteeth, his face red, making soft oofing noises, people screaming . . .

My muscles were locked. I saw his face, at the end of my arms, turning blue. My fingers were round his throat. I felt his fingers prying uselessly at mine. He was twitching. I didn't see any of the people screaming. I heard gibbering and did just see, out of the corner of my eye, Wa Yatsimura trotting toward me, raising a length of pipe. I turned and started—but only started—

to raise my arm. Then I went visiting in a land where the trees hang with cauliflower and lotus blossoms fill the air.

"Joe," said the old man, sitting next to my hospital bed, "you're the finest field agent I've had in twenty years in Weights and Measures. You don't know how hard it is for me to say this."

"Then don't," I mumbled through my bandages. They'd wrapped my head up pretty good—and had needed to, as much as Wa Yatsimura had worked on it before the police managed to drag him off.

"There were witnesses, Joe. They all said you attacked the Jap. You're lucky he's not filing a criminal complaint."

"Check his scales. They're piped."

"We already did. They're clean, Joe."

"Then he's a thumb weigher. The Yatsimuras are dirty, Fred. I can't tell you how I know, but I do."

The old man took off his glasses, breathed on them, started wiping them with his tie. He wasn't looking at me when he said, "You've taken state regulations into your own hands. I'll need your plastic, Joe." I thought there were tears in his eyes.

I know there were tears in mine.

When I checked out three days later my head was still bandaged, but I was able to drive. The old man, or someone, had arranged to have my car brought over to the hospital in the Valley. I was fighting rush hour so it was early evening by the time I got to Brentwood, dazed from the drive, from being out in the world.

The neighborhood was cool. As I stepped out of my car the palms and jacarandas rustled in the breeze. The door slam echoed crisply up the street. I was sweaty from the drive and hadn't shaved in three days. I must have been a sight, if anyone was looking—my jaw dark with stubble, my head swathed in white.

I leaned against the car and looked at her house. The lights were just starting to go on along the street, though none did in her place. It was a Jap design, with rich, low-slung wood, its eave a long arcing brow. The house looked out darkly, placidly, over the gentle rise of lawn, like a ship perched on a rolling wave. Redwood fence dropped away from either side to enclose its back garden. Faintly, very faintly, I thought I heard its fountain gurgle.

I folded my arms, leaning against the car, watching the house that seemed mutely to watch me. My head itched under the bandages. The breeze stiffened and crawled through my hair where it poofed out on top. Sounding like a seashell at the beach, the breeze murmured in the bandages over my ears, and it grew cold as I stood there and hugged myself, waiting, I don't know how long, I don't know what for. Maybe I was waiting for Miss Ohara, or for any woman, to open the door, invite me in, rub my feet, and take the pain from my heart.

I stood there as it grew dark.

THE OLD BOYS

We hear the intermittent muted click-clack of a distant billiard game and, somewhat closer, murmuring male voices engaged in separate conversations.

Closer still is the crackle of a fire.

Very present is the rustle of a newspaper page being turned.

After a beat, another page is turned.

After another beat:

VOICE: Ah, Bridger. Are you eating?

A nearing voice:

BRIDGER: Hallo, Soames. No, thanks, I take very little in the evenings nowadays.

SOAMES: Yes? Quite certain? Rump roast.

There is the thump and hiss of a body settling into a leather-cushioned chair.

BRIDGER: Is it *Thurs*day.

SOAMES: Mm.

BRIDGER: Rump roast. Mm. But the thing about that is—

SOAMES: Ah yes, you had the intestine out, didn't you.

BRIDGER: Mm. Small intestine. Still, rump roast.

SOAMES: Mm.

BRIDGER: Well I might be persuaded. I might be persuaded. (the rustle of a newspaper being picked up) . . . What's the word on the new man?

SOAMES: Name is Pim Phipps-Phillips. They say he's quite the chap.

BRIDGER: Pim Phipps-Phillips. Not Harry Phipps-Phillips's boy?

SOAMES: Mm.

BRIDGER: Mm. With Agatha?

SOAMES: No. The second one.

BRIDGER: Althea.

SOAMES: No, she was third. Agape.

BRIDGER: Ah yes, the Ta Hitian woman.

SOAMES: Mm. No—Greek. You're thinking of Amahoke.

BRIDGER: Ah yes. Quite right. Mm. A Levantine.

SOAMES: Pim? Mm.

BRIDGER: An Hellene.

SOAMES: Mm. Well—demi. Hellenic.

BRIDGER: Strange name, what.

SOAMES: Mm.

BRIDGER: Pim.

SOAMES: Has to do with the circumstances of his conception. It seems that Harry and the Greek woman had been drinking Pimm's cups.

BRIDGER: Number Seven?

SOAMES: Seven? Was it Seven? Don't know the number. I expect it might have been.

BRIDGER: Mm. I'd expect so.

SOAMES: Mm. A child eventuating.

BRIDGER: Mm.

SOAMES: Anyway, he's quite the man for the job.

BRIDGER: Oh, I don't doubt that. Of course—what *is* the job?

SOAMES: You have me there. (A gong sounds.) . . . Right. Rump roast.

Two bodies are hoisting themselves out of club chairs.

BRIDGER: Ah, Thursdays.

Later, elsewhere. Muted traffic; with the sound of a door opening, we hear a typewriter close by.

SOAMES: Phipps-Phillips?

PIM: Sir.

SOAMES: Do come in. Chair, et cetera.

PIM: Thank you, sir.

As the door closes the typing becomes muted.

SOAMES: I hear you're quite the fellow.

PIM: Sir?

SOAMES: Oh yes. Oh yes—quite the chap.

PIM: Well sir, I hope—

SOAMES: Harry's boy, I hear.

PIM: Yes sir. Though I never knew him.

SOAMES: Ah yes. Wouldn't have, would you?

PIM: No sir.

SOAMES: Traipsing off to Ta Hiti.

PIM: Kuala Lumpur.

SOAMES: K.L.? But surely—Amahoke—

PIM: K.L. for a number of years, then Tahiti.

SOAMES: . . . *Is* that right.

PIM: Yes sir.

SOAMES: My point was that, eventually, he found himself in Ta Hiti.

PIM: Yes sir. Of course.

SOAMES: One doesn't claim to be exhaustive.

PIM: Of course sir. I'm sorry.

SOAMES: One isn't the encyclopedia.

PIM: No sir. Of course not. I'm very sorry.

SOAMES: Mm.

A beat. Soames clears his throat.

SOAMES: . . . Well then. You know what the job is, I take it.

PIM: No sir.

SOAMES: . . . You *don't* know what the job is.

PIM: No sir.

SOAMES: You have no idea what the job is.

PIM: No sir. No idea.

SOAMES: You—you expect me to tell you what the job is?

PIM: Well—yes sir. Or—whatever you please. If someone else is meant to tell me, if that's the, uh—

SOAMES: Well someone else had damned well better!

A beat.

SOAMES: . . . Hadn't they!

PIM: Yes sir. As you please.

SOAMES: Because I don't know!

PIM: . . . I, uh—

SOAMES: Do I!

PIM: No sir.

SOAMES: Right. Right.

A beat. Soames clears his throat.

SOAMES: . . . Now, come back to me when you've been properly briefed.

PIM: Yes sir.

SOAMES: And tell me what the job is.

PIM: Of course sir.

SOAMES: Or perhaps you think your supervisor needn't *know* what you're doing.

PIM: Uh . . .

SOAMES: Eh, Phipps-Phillips!

PIM: No sir, uh . . .

SOAMES: Speak up, boy!

PIM: Of course you should know what I'm doing, sir. As my supervisor.

SOAMES: But I don't, do I?

Pim: No sir. But I meant, you're entitled to know, once I myself know, sir.

Soames: Really! How kind of you!

Pim: No—no sir, I just—uh, one rather thought you *did* know.

Soames: Well then one was wrong, wasn't one!

Pim: Yes sir. I'm sorry, sir. Oh dear. I'm off on the wrong foot, aren't I.

Soames: Very well. That's all, Phipps-Phillips.

A chair creaks, relieved of weight.

Pim: I'm sorry, sir.

Soames: Hm.

Once again we hear the distant click of billiard balls, the murmur of male voices, a crackling fire.

There is the thump and hiss of a body seating itself in a leather chair followed very shortly by a second thump and hiss.

There is the scratch and sputter of a match being lit, then the creak of leather as a body leans forward, then the breathy lip-pops of a cigar being sucked to life.

BRIDGER: 'K you.

SOAMES: Mm.

The ping of the match into an ashtray; the sputter of a second match being lit; the popping inhales of a second cigar lighting; the ping of the second match in the ashtray.

Occasional puffing.

At length:

BRIDGER: One wonders, in retrospect, about the brisket.

SOAMES: Mm.

More puffs.

BRIDGER: . . . Is that Roofrose?

SOAMES: Mm?

BRIDGER: In the corner there?

SOAMES: By the uh, asleep there?

BRIDGER: Is he asleep?

SOAMES: Or perhaps that's . . . Isn't Roofrose over in . . .

BRIDGER: I believe it is Roofrose.

SOAMES: Hm.

More puffing.

BRIDGER: How's the new man shaping up?

SOAMES: Phipps-Phillips.

BRIDGER: Mm.

SOAMES: Disappointment.

BRIDGER: Really.

SOAMES: Mm.

BRIDGER: Oh dear.

SOAMES: Yes.

BRIDGER: One wouldn't expect Harry Phipps-Phillips's boy to be a disappointment.

SOAMES: And it is there precisely that he disappoints.

BRIDGER: Odd.

SOAMES: Mm.

BRIDGER: Dullard?

SOAMES: No . . . No, Pim.

BRIDGER: Yes but, mentally, is he—

SOAMES: Oh. . . . No, I shouldn't say so. Closemouthed.

BRIDGER: *Harry's* boy?

SOAMES: Mm. Had the very devil of a time getting it out of him, what the job was. And the lad trod bloody close to insubordination.

BRIDGER: Well—youth.

SOAMES: Yes, I suppose. Still.

BRIDGER: Well of course.

SOAMES: Mm.

BRIDGER: What *was* the job?

SOAMES: Hm? Oh. Rather routine as it turns out. Nip in, nip out. Bulgaria, I believe. Sofia, what.

BRIDGER: Ah yes, Sofia.

SOAMES: Man to shoot.

BRIDGER: Hm. Bulgarian?

SOAMES: Mm.

BRIDGER: Well, that would be the place for it.

SOAMES: Mm . . . Yes. Yes, I believe you're right. I believe that is Roofrose.

BRIDGER: Mm.

SOAMES: Brandy?

BRIDGER: Hm. Well . . . It might settle the, uh . . .

SOAMES: Mm. Steward!

A distant foghorn. Footsteps on paving stones.

SOAMES: Phipps-Phillips?

PIM: Sir? Is that you?

SOAMES: What's this all about, boy?

PIM: —Who is that?!

SOAMES: You know bloody well who it is!

PIM: No! Behind you, that horrible man!

SOAMES: How the devil should I know? Someone walking his dog.

PIM: Were you followed?

SOAMES: Don't be daft. What's going on? What's the idea, meeting out here?

PIM: The Bulgarians are after me!

SOAMES: Oh bollocks.

PIM: Yes sir!

SOAMES: Don't be a fool, boy, no one's after you.

PIM: I shot the Bulgarian!

SOAMES: Well yes, good show, but let's put it in perspective, lad, Bulgarians are shot every—well, perhaps not every day, but certainly the odd Bulgarian is shot every, oh—

PIM: Yes sir, but—

SOAMES: I mean it's hardly shooting the albatross. All part of the game, really—we ping away at one of theirs, they poke one of ours with a poisoned umbrella tip—no one takes it personally.

PIM: No sir, but—

SOAMES: And it's not as if we're in danger of running out of them. If the odd Bulgie has to be liquidated now and again, reasons of state, Her Majesty, what have you, well, that's why the good Lord made so many.

PIM: Yes sir, I quite agree, but—

SOAMES: So let's pull our socks up, go home, get some sleep—knit the raveled sleeve, what—and discuss it at work tomorrow if we have any nagging little worries.

PIM: Yes sir, but—

SOAMES: There's a lad, there's a jolly good agent—off we go!

PIM: (retreating) All right sir. Well—thank you.

SOAMES: Oh tosh. There's a lad!

Once again, the distant click of billiards, murmuring voices, crackling fire. A newspaper page is turned.

A long beat.

SOAMES: . . . Oh, pity.

BRIDGER: Hm?

SOAMES: Gray-crested grebe . . . reduced numbers. Winter breeding grounds encroached . . . development, mmmshopping . . .

BRIDGER: Oh, pity.

Another page is turned.

BRIDGER: . . . New man getting the hang of things?

SOAMES: Oh, quite the contrary I'm afraid. Quite wet.

BRIDGER: Oh dear.

SOAMES: No nerve. Sad.

BRIDGER: Oh dear. Made a hash of the job?

SOAMES: No no, did the job.

BRIDGER: Yes?

SOAMES: Then fell rather to pieces. Imagined the Bulgarians were after him. Poor beggar.

BRIDGER: Mm. Having to let him go then?

SOAMES: No.

BRIDGER: Ah—another chance, a little seasoning?

SOAMES: No.

Another page is turned.

SOAMES: . . . No, he uh . . . died.

BRIDGER: Really.

SOAMES: Yes. Poisoned umbrella prick.

BRIDGER: Ah . . . Where?

SOAMES: . . . Buttock, I imagine?

BRIDGER: Yes but, Sofia, or—

SOAMES: No no, Westminster Bridge. Shortly after I talked to him, it seems.

BRIDGER: *Quel ironie.*

SOAMES: Yes.

BRIDGER: They *were* after him.

SOAMES: Yes. But of course he had no way of knowing.

BRIDGER: Yes of course. Silly to think—even if events should bear him out, uh . . . Well, the man was green.

SOAMES: Mm.

BRIDGER: Still—pity.

SOAMES: Oh yes. Always regrettable . . .

Another page is turned. Absently:

SOAMES: . . . Always regrettable . . .

Muted traffic. A door opens.

DEBANZIE: Ah, Soames, do sit down. (A chair scrapes.) Hear we lost a man.

SOAMES: Yes sir.

DEBANZIE: This new chap we sent after the Bulgarian.

SOAMES: Yes. Pim Phipps-Phillips.

DEBANZIE: Not Harry's boy?

SOAMES: Yes, I'm afraid.

DEBANZIE: Mm. Well we've lodged a strong complaint.

SOAMES: Hear hear, sir.

DEBANZIE: Don't expect much will come of it.

SOAMES: Probably not, sir.

DEBANZIE: It was retaliation, of course. It seems this Bulgarian we'd had him squidge was a nephew of Todor Zhivkov's.

SOAMES: Yes, so I was told.

DEBANZIE: Did you warn the lad?

SOAMES: . . . Sir?

DEBANZIE: That his target was . . . connected?

SOAMES: *Was* he, sir?

DEBANZIE: Well, as I say, nephew of Zhivkov.

SOAMES: And . . . Zhivkov is . . . ?

DEBANZIE: Runs the place.

SOAMES: Mm. . . . And what place would that be, sir?

DEBANZIE: Bulgaria.

SOAMES: Really.

DEBANZIE: Oh yes.

SOAMES: I was told he was secretary.

DEBANZIE: Yes well, that's what they call the chap who runs the place.

SOAMES: Well really. Shouldn't they call him prime minister or premier or—or—I don't know—something firsty?

DEBANZIE: Mm.

SOAMES: I'd no idea. "Nephew of Secretary Zhivkov"—thought his uncle was a functionary. Head of their . . . geographic society or some such. I mean "secretary," sounds a bit gray, what; how are people meant to know?

DEBANZIE: Mm.

SOAMES: The whole point of bureaucracy is chain of command I should think, clear lines of authority. Head of state—secretary? A bit Irish, isn't it, sir?

DEBANZIE: Mm.

SOAMES: I wonder they sort anything.

DEBANZIE: Well some say they don't, the Bulgarians.

SOAMES: I don't wonder!

DEBANZIE: Shooting the pope, so on.

SOAMES: . . . They didn't.

DEBANZIE: Oh yes, last year.

SOAMES: And—he died?

DEBANZIE: No. Recovered. Still—pontiff.

SOAMES: I should say.

DEBANZIE: Catholics can't have been pleased.

SOAMES: Mm.

DEBANZIE: And now Harry's boy . . . Yes, Todor Zhivkov. Not a pleasant fellow, from what I gather. Small, vindictive. Hard cheese on Harry's boy. (A phone rings, a handset is unpronged.) Yes? . . . Sure . . . Sure, the St. James? . . . Hang on. (viva voce) Very well, Soames. Thank you. Chin up. Carry on.

SOAMES: Sir.

A chair scrapes.

Crackling fire; billiards.

ROOFROSE: Ah, hallo Soames.

SOAMES: Roofrose. Thought you were in—what was it? Cameroon?

ROOFROSE: Was. Back now. Shall I move the paper?

SOAMES: No no. Seen Bridger?

ROOFROSE: Yes in fact and—you just missed Harry.

SOAMES: Harry?

ROOFROSE: Phipps-Phillips.

SOAMES: *Here*? Not here. *Here*?

ROOFROSE: Yes, he was looking for his boy, uh—Pim, is it?

A beat.

There is the crackle of newspaper and the rumple of leather as a body drops heavily into a club chair. There is a long, long hiss as the cushion expels air.

Finally:

SOAMES: Really.

ROOFROSE: Yes. Time has not been kind to Harry. Leprous, I daresay, and other gnawing diseases. Tropical, venereal, effluvial. Bits of his nose hanging off, husky voice, doddering gait. One wondered, where are the bells of Notre Dame?

SOAMES: Really.

ROOFROSE: And what a tale of woe; Bridger and I were mesmerized. He'd been round Tahiti, the Celibes, Kuala Lumpur, and other points East. Steamers, cane chairs, hotel verandas. And female liaisons galore—well, you know Harry. Recorded more marriages than intervening divorces. Local norms offended, an awkwardness, and then he'd move on. Drink, gambling, and a terrible soul-shattering loneliness for all that he roistered and spread his seed. Finally fetched up in Sebastopol cadging drinks from Russian sailors. Derelict in a foreign port—you know how these things go—he was recruited by the DS.

SOAMES: DS?

ROOFROSE: Bulgarian secret police. Poor chap. Porous brain, wrung for whatever it retained concerning British Intelligence. They kept him on as a consulting asset. Can't imagine he was much use to them. Cruel devils. They finally agreed to send him back to England on condition he do one last job—they needed someone who knew London. Fellow to kill. Gave him an umbrella. Nasty business. But Harry was desperate to come back so as to see his son once before he died.

SOAMES: (dully) Yes. I see.

ROOFROSE: I didn't know what to tell him; haven't seen his boy. Poignant story, though, and Bridger—heavens!—the man was overcome! Sobbing! Remarkable thing. He staggered off to the bar; you might find him there. But Harry's left. The porter came round just moments ago to chase him off. Disturbing the members, he said, moaning and drooling on the rugs and so forth. I managed to tuck a fiver in his pocket as he shambled away. Hope he finds his boy. Strange name—Pim. Wonder how Harry came to give it to him. I say—Soames? Are you all right? . . . I say—Soames?

RED WING

I know. Alls ya see is a body in the yard there and ya figure, well someone sure did a number on *her*. Head missin' and everything. Just her neck stump there, with all that mess snaggling out of it, the arteries, the, uh, I guess that's the windpipe there, the what have you. I guess it's natural, ya think *she's* the victim. Heck, I would too, if that was all I seen. If I didn't know what led up to it. The way she rode me and all. And she rode me pretty good. You better believe it. She rode me pretty darn good. Not that I'm sayin', uh, you know. The end don't justify the means, or whatever. It was just pretty goddamn grim is *my* point.

Well ya say okay, so she rode ya. She gave ya a hard time. Still that don't justify no head missin'. Sure, that's how most people will see it—I'm not a dummy here. I know how it looks. The eustachian tube. Yah. That's what it is.

Anyway. I'm just sayin'.

Look from the other side.

I mean, picture *this*. So we're lyin' in bed one night and she puts her arm around me. And she starts rubbin' around. And I shrug it off 'cause I'm not in the mood, see. Like it happens. Ya can't always be in the mood. So I shrug it off and she says, Well I guess it's true what they say.

And I says, So what do they say?

And she says, That the fruit don't fall far from the tree.

And I says, What's that supposed to mean?

And she says, Ya know darn well what it means.

And I says, Supposen ya tell me?

And she says, By his fruit shall ye know him.

And I says, Proverbs, proverbs.

And she says, Well how would you explain it then?

And I says, Explain what?

And she says, Kyle going gay.

Our boy Kyle, he lives up in Minneapolis, and he told us fifteen months ago he's gone gay. Now this is not something, for proper people, this is not something ya drag into a marital dispute. This is a source of heartache and soul-searching I can tell you. This is our boy here, and not a, uh, not a piece a ammunition for some, you know. This is not something ya use to make a damn mud pie. It's something we never even discussed, though we shed some tears, I can tell you. So now it makes me angry.

And then she says more.

Maybe, she says, maybe you prefer sticking your thing in Norm Wollensky's big old butt.

Now this is way out into the realm of I don't know what. Norm Wollensky, he's a friend of mine, it's true. And we ice fish together, if that's a crime, which I am not aware that it is. But

Norm and me, Christ, we barely even talk to each other. I'll say to him, Norm, how are ya for a little fishin' this weekend, and he'll say Yah, and I'll drive go pick him up and then we barely talk on the way out to Mille Lacs and hardly even say a word once we're out there in the hut fishing except maybe, Whoa, there's one, or, Whoa, is that one?

So this, she's going beyond, this is plain old goat getting, and it's childish and I say it's garbage.

But later that night, afterwards, just to prove to myself that it's garbage, I sit there and, not that I would tell this to anyone, but I sat and shut my eyes and imagined Norm Wollensky taking off his trousers. Real slow, his back to me. And then he drops his briefs. And then he steps slowly out of his briefs. And then, with his back still to me, he leans forward and puts his hands on his knees, and he waggles his behind. And let me tell you—honestly—nothing. There was no feeling of a sexual nature provoked within me. And I know people say, well, we never really know, even about ourselves, I mean you may be married forty years and then molest an eight-year-old, because the sexual desire will well up from within. Just hit a gusher. But I am telling you. I am about as interested in Norm Wollensky's butt as, well I just can't even imagine. And I tried to picture it as vivid as I could, him dropping the trousers and so forth, with nice light, but I cannot conceive of the physical act of putting my thing in Norm's butt. And anyway, what would Norm be doing meanwhile? But these imaginings was later. At the time I just says to her, Well that's pathetic.

And then she says, *I'll* say it is, and rolls over as if she's won the argument. Which leaves me fuming.

Except there's more even, because after a minute the bed is shaking so I can tell she's cryin'. And she's making sounds, little ones, nothing showy, just enough to let me know. As if *I've* hurt *her* feelings by talking about *her* sticking *her* thing which she doesn't even have into Norm Wollensky's behind, and now I'm supposed to apologize to *her* which makes *no* damn sense. And this is her, this is my wife, this is her right to the ground, making me always in the wrong. This is what drives me so crazy. This—she lies there crying, with me so angry I can't see straight. This is what I'm driving at.

And was that the only time? No sir, that was not the only time. Like we're lying in bed once and she says, So then, uh, what did you think of Arne Carlson?

And I says, Not a bad governor.

And Rudy Perpich? she says.

And I'm wondering but I says, Not too bad.

And she says, So how come we didn't get to have sex during either a their administrations?

Now this is pure poppycock, it's beyond exaggeration, and I says, Ya don't know what you're talkin' about, that's a lot of damn shit I says, and I don't use that word frequently. Damn I do but not the other one.

Not since Al Quie! she says. Not since Al Quie!

A lot of damn shit, I says.

You're goddamn right it is! she says, and rolls over. But I can tell it's not gonna end there, that she hasn't had enough yet and she's just lying there thinking.

And sure enough in two minutes she rolls back over and

says, I guess you think it's pretty funny, gettin' into arguments like this.

And I says, I don't think it's funny.

Well you do it enough, she says.

And I don't say nothing.

If you don't like it how come you do it all the time? she says. I think you do like it.

And I don't say nothing.

And then I says, Do what now?

And she says, Huh?

And I says, You say I do it all the time.

And she says, Yeah, as if you enjoy it, like you think it's funny.

And I says, But do what now? What do I do?

And she says, Oh for God's sake!

And that's that. But then after a few minutes, just when I'm drifting off, she says, You know if it wasn't for the financial practicalities I would just move out. And I don't say nothin' so she says, I would move out s'darned fast it'd make your head spin.

So I think about it and then I think about it and then I say, Well, we can talk about the financials.

Oho says she, Yah sure we can talk. Talk about two households on what you make. A long darn talk that'll be.

Then another minute.

Well, she says, maybe I could go live with Kyle.

And I says, Now you're not gonna do that. I'm thinkin', for Christ sakes, the boy has a life up there in the Twin Cities, and it may not be the life we would a chosen for him but it ain't the sulfury fires of hell neither which is what her bein' down there would make it for him.

And she says, It would just be temporary, while I get my bearings.

And I says, Now that boy has a life there, and it may not be, it may not be, uh, it may not—

And she says, Kyle would love to see me for a little while.

And I says, Now—

And she says, You don't even know your own boy. He would love it.

And I says, Now I know that boy—

And she says, Yah well that would explain all the times you predicted him going gay. I guess you know him real good. Maybe I'll stay up there, she says. With Kyle.

Well she ends up not calling him but goddamnit now she knows how to get me going. So she keeps talkin' about movin' in with Kyle. Just to make my gut churn.

So she's churnin' my gut on a daily basis. And this is when she starts goin' on the shopping trips with her friend Connie.

Now I don't care for Connie. Connie is a woman she could be a linebacker if ladies with hot flashes ever formed a league. She wears gold bangles and these shirts with the flashy prints that she can't quite fit into that they make out of a fabric that goes SHEEK-SHEEK-SHEEK whenever she walks around with her big old arms swinging. These shirts, I'm tellin' ya, you hold a match within five yards and WOOMPH! that would be the end of Connie Buchanan. Like in a forest fire, when the next tree in line just bursts into flame. And her head would go too because, believe me, that big puffy white hair is mostly air and hair spray and would just go WOOMPH! so there she'd be, a big greasy naked thing all charred except with gold bangles still hanging around her wrists and those big green eyeglasses melted all over her black blubbery nose and smoke wisping off the top of her head.

WOOMPH!

So like I say, I don't care for Connie. She's loud and she smokes so that I can always smell if she's been in the house when I walk in even if she hasn't lit up because of the damned perfume. And she's in the house more and more, cackling and walking around and smoking, and then they go out shopping, the two of them, more than they ever did before. And my wife now, when she asks for money she calls it her Settlement. This is from our discussions about Kyle, because she said once Well okay if I'm not going to move in with Kyle then you've got to give me a Settlement.

And I said What do you mean a Settlement?

And she said, Well things can't just go on like they are; this marriage is dead and you've got to give me a Settlement.

Which meant that things *did* just go on like they were except that she spent more and more money and called it a Settlement. And she'd not only go out shopping but Connie also got her started going to the Indian casino a couple times a week. And I work for NSP, I am not Mr. J. P. Morgan. And she even started talking louder, like Connie. This is not my imagination. It was like she busted free all of a sudden, except that makes it sound like a good thing. She was free in a bad way, like all her life she'd just been waiting for an opportunity to turn into Connie Buchanan and start buying them ugly print shirts.

And I said once, All this money you're spending, you ever think about our retirement?

And she'd say, What do you mean?

And I said, It's not just my money, it's *our* money your throwin' away here.

And she said, Well, you should a thought a that before.

And I said, Before what?

And she said Oh for Pete's sake and walked away like I was a goddamn idiot.

But I couldn't not give her the money because then she'd just start in on Kyle and "our marriage is dead" and what have you. It was blackmail, see. Nothing more than damn blackmail. Because we both knew if I didn't give her the Settlement then she would bring up how I couldn't, uh, didn't have the sexual, uh, hadn't been engaging in the sex act. That was always in the background. The threat of her being ready to blab about all this stuff that I don't think needs to be talked about. And she'd waltz around the subject, just to churn my gut. She'd even hint about it with Connie there, and come up to me in front of Connie and demand her Settlement. It made no difference for her to boss me around with someone right there. And once I heard Connie say to *her*, Why don't you get some of your Settlement from that lump in the living room? which made me suspect it was even possible the whole idea came from Connie.

And then once in front of Norm, we were playing cards and she asked me for her Settlement, so I give her some money and she leaves and Norm says, What did she mean, Settlement?

And I said Aw, nothin'.

That's how bad it was.

But it was worse, really; I don't know if I can describe it. See, she was makin' it impossible for me to have, you know, sex relations with her, by using it as a thing to beat me up with. Like if I did try to have sex relations, that would mean she had won and I was giving up, and it would a been the occasion for a lot of smug remarks. So just thinking about that made it impossible for me to have sex relations. I mean the sex act, it's supposed to be about things that, uh, two people—you know, not things of, not winning or losing or beating someone, the sex act, the fleshly thing that, uh, the holy joy of, ya know, the celebration that—well, it just wasn't right. And she was wrecking it and using it for goddamn money. My own wife was using sex for goddamn money, and was grinding me into the muck. Right into the damn muck. And the more she ground me into the muck, the better she seemed to feel.

And she made me smaller and smaller and smaller, and she got bigger and bigger, and bought more and more horrible shirts and started to go casino gambling *three* times a week. And she ground me into the muck. And she stood upon me so that she herself would not be in the muck. My own wife stood upon me, in the muck.

That's what I mean.

And the life force drained from me, and went into her. Our future flowed into her in the form of our retirement money. And our present flowed into her in the form of my vital spirit. And our past ceased to be. For she was a different person. And I was a husk.

And people noticed. Kyle, even. I was talking to him on the phone one day and he said, Jeez, Mom seems to have come into her own. That's what he said, she's come into her own, like it was a good thing. And I said, Yah, ya think? Because I could not tell the boy that his own mother had become a muck-grinding giantess and had even threatened to make his own life a muddy hell. You cannot tell that to a boy.

So people noticed. About her, I mean, not about me. They did not notice that I had become a husk, maybe because I am not the demonstrative type. Maybe I always seemed like a husk. Although once at work Fred Martins said, Jeez, are you okay? I said, Yah. Also, I forgot, Norm Wollensky said once, after I turned down a second fishing trip in a row he said, Well . . . okay. As if to say, Well, I don't understand, but I'm not gonna pry.

And I appreciated that.

But ordinarily, people did not notice.

They did not notice how big she had become. She was as big as an elephant, a great mad elephant trampling madly through the village of our life, knocking over all the little thatched huts and chasing the natives who ran screaming before her until they got mashed between her stubby wriggling toes. I had no power before this mad elephant. My power had drained away, so I stared, stupefied, as she charged trumpeting this way and that, to the shopping mall, to the Indian casino, to Connie Buchanan's Kaffee Klatsch which was what she left me a note one day saying she was at so I should fix my own dinner. And the wind whistled where all the thatched huts had been, but now stood only the odd tumbled chimminey, wisping smoke.

. . .

I don't remember the act itself. The first thing I remember is running through the woods, making loud hunking noises as I tried to breathe. My gut was bouncing and my lungs stung with sharp air. My chest ached as if there was an old fan blade inside clattering against my ribs. Time was, I could run and run and run on forward-flowing feet. Now my footfalls were big up-and-down crashes that shook the ground and jangled my spine. Time was, nothing on me bounced. Now everything heaved and jostled, and my insides slurped this way and that. I realized there was something laced through the fingers of my right hand, from which swung some weight. Her hair, her head.

Before that sometimes, in bed, I had trouble breathing. She would sleep there beside me breathing in and out, in and out, like a big industrial compressor. But I could not breathe. I would lie staring at the ceiling, staring at the squashed-flat ceiling, night after night. I lay there with my fists clenched, body rigid and squashed flat, like I was being forced down into the mattress by stones, stones that had been rolled onto my chest, stones so heavy I could not breathe. Next to me the great bellows went in and out, in and out, untroubled to eternity.

One night she rolls over towards me and her eyes open up. She looks at me and after a minute she says, "For Pete's sake—go to *sleep*!" Then she rolls over and starts breathing again, in and out, in and out.

. . .

I sat against a tree in the cool autumn. My breathing slowed to normal, and in the woods was a great peace. I wanted the moment of peace to last forever, the moment before thought and planning would have to resume. Here there was peace, and breathing, and the moment. Beyond the moment would only be pain. So the moment was ringed round with fear, and it was important to stay inside the moment. We had been young once, and in love. She was a demure girl from the iron range. And now her head lay beside me in the leaves. It was a time for reflection.

I do not know how long the moment was. It was its own time, for time had stopped. And then the moment ended, and time and fear resumed.

I was running through the woods again. I thought, maybe I can stay with Kyle. Up in the Twin Cities. But then I thought, could I really stay in his apartment, sit on the couch and be innerduced to his young gay friends and sip wine and sit and chat about matters of the day? Would I fit in—or would it be awkward? And would I bring his mother's head? No, this was exactly her way of thinking. You cannot burden your own child like that.

Yes, now I remember, right after, flinging the hatchet away. It went whippity-whoosh into the woods. Then I guess I started running.

Our lives were together really. This act, it was not meant to separate her life from mine. It was crazy, granted. But not that way, not to separate myself. That much is clear to me as I walk through the woods now, still holding on to her. I would tell her this if she could hear. Like when a plant gradually grows around a stake in the garden, after a while you just cannot separate it. Not that one of us was the plant and one the stake. Like two plants that grow and twist around one another and one just ends up choking the other off. They didn't separate, one just choked off. It got tighter and tighter until the one couldn't breathe. Or the other. They choked off, or maybe they got too heavy and flumped to the ground, into the shade. And then trees grew around them, new trees, that stretched up out of the shade and into the light. This would be Kyle, I guess. I'm not quite sure how the homo thing fits in.

Maybe I'm thinking this way because I am walking through the woods and the trees stretch up. It has grown twilight, and chill. I am just walking now; I do not know how it will end. Oh my dear Jesus, I feel so very lost.

ABOUT THE AUTHOR

ETHAN COEN is the Samuel Gelbfisz Professor of English as a Second Language at the University of Colorado at Boulder. He is the author of *Homeward Plods: Images of the Cowswain in 18th Century Verse*, and *For Art's Sake: Schopenhauer's Esthetics*. He is married to the percussionist Grace Buller-Gorge, whose husband Sir Hugh Ayrehead-Maybe of the Austin-Davies Ayrehead-Maybes is Chief Disciplinarian of the Glamorgan Male Choir. They have two children, Alun and Gwynff, as does he. Coen is an accomplished nudist and is the author of a study of Scott's *Kenilworth* which was universally ignored, as well as of three volumes of poetry or, if any publisher should prefer, one big one.